SYDNEY'

The world has witnessed everything from the sublime to the ridiculous while watching the decades-old feud between the world's richest gem dealers, the Blackstones, and the Hammonds. But yesterday's scene tops even that. Blackstones' exclusive supermodel, Briana Davenport—the "Face of Blackstone"—was seen on the arm of none other than supposed enemy Jarrod Hammond.

The two were spotted together at the roulette table in the Crown Casino last week, and yesterday at the Melbourne Grand Prix. "They looked to be a *lot* more than friends," said one attentive attendee.

According to an inside source, Danvenport's contract with Blackstones is soon to be up for renewal. Locking lips with a Hammond may not be Davenport's best move to ensure longevity with the diamond moguls. Then again, she may not care, if the consolation prize is the sexy Melbourne millionaire. One thing's for sure: At Blackstones, the flawless diamonds may be costly, but the family hijinks are priceless.

Dear Reader,

When I sold my first book to the Silhouette Desire line back in January 2006, the senior editor, Melissa Jeglinski, commented that the Down Under Desire authors should put a continuity series together—and the DIAMONDS DOWN UNDER series was born.

With much enthusiasm we set about coming up with story lines. I'd always wanted to write an indecent-proposal story, and this glitter and glamour series was the perfect backdrop for that. I really enjoyed writing about a hero who desires the heroine so much he is prepared to pay her a million dollars to sleep with him. Now that's desire!

I had a great time with this book, and I'm so proud to have worked with such talented writers. Writing this series bonded us not only in friendship, but also as a "family" of authors. And, yes, a family who has arguments and who want to strangle each other at times. ☺ But I wouldn't have missed out on this for anything.

I hope you enjoy our series. Personally, I think it's fabulous.

Happy reading!

Maxine

MAXINE
SULLIVAN

MISTRESS & A MILLION DOLLARS

Silhouette®
Desire

Published by Silhouette Books
America's Publisher of Contemporary Romance

To Melissa Jeglinski for "everything."
To the Down Under Desire authors—with admiration.

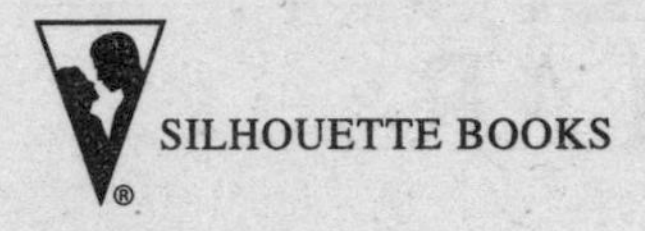

ISBN-13: 978-0-373-76855-4
ISBN-10: 0-373-76855-9

MISTRESS & A MILLION DOLLARS

This edition published by arrangement with Harlequin Books S.A.

Visit Silhouette Books at www.eHarlequin.com

Printed in U.S.A.

Books by Maxine Sullivan

Silhouette Desire

**The Millionaire's Seductive Revenge* #1782
**The Tycoon's Blackmailed Mistress* #1800
**The Executive's Vengeful Seduction* #1818
Mistress & a Million Dollars #1855

*Australian Millionaires

MAXINE SULLIVAN

credits her mother for her lifelong love of romance novels, so it was a natural extension for Maxine to want to write her own romances. She's very excited about seeing her work in print and is thrilled to be the second Australian to write for the Silhouette Desire line.

Maxine lives in Melbourne, Australia, and over the years has traveled to New Zealand, the U.K. and the U.S.A. In her own backyard, her husband's job ensured they saw the diversity of the countryside, including spending many years in Darwin in the tropical north, where some of her books are set. She is married to Geoff, who has proven his hero-status many times over the years. They have two handsome sons and an assortment of much-loved, previously abandoned animals.

Maxine would love to hear from you and can be contacted through her Web site at www.maxinesullivan.com.

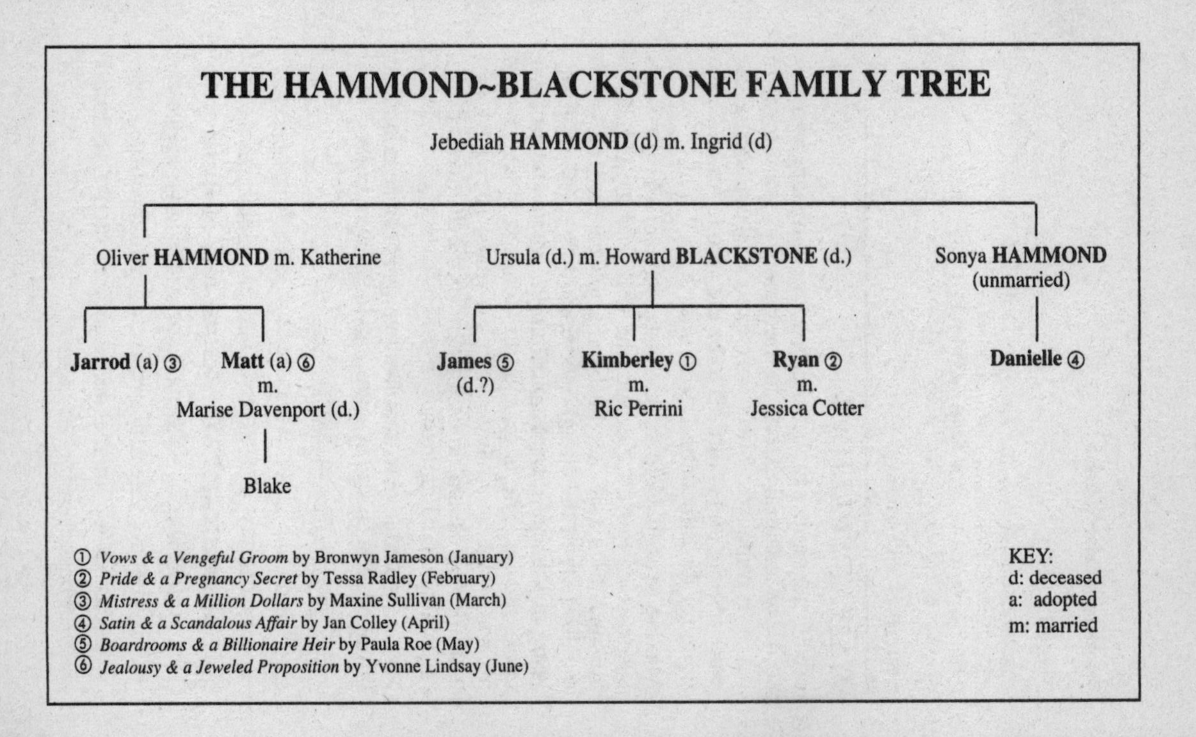
THE HAMMOND~BLACKSTONE FAMILY TREE
Jebediah HAMMOND (d) m. Ingrid (d)
Oliver HAMMOND m. Katherine
Ursula (d.) m. Howard BLACKSTONE (d.)
Sonya HAMMOND (unmarried)
Jarrod (a) ③
Matt (a) ⑥ m. Marise Davenport (d.)
Blake
James ⑤ (d.?)
Kimberley ① m. Ric Perrini
Ryan ② m. Jessica Cotter
Danielle ④
① Vows & a Vengeful Groom by Bronwyn Jameson (January)
② Pride & a Pregnancy Secret by Tessa Radley (February)
③ Mistress & a Million Dollars by Maxine Sullivan (March)
④ Satin & a Scandalous Affair by Jan Colley (April)
⑤ Boardrooms & a Billionaire Heir by Paula Roe (May)
⑥ Jealousy & a Jeweled Proposition by Yvonne Lindsay (June)
KEY:
d: deceased
a: adopted
m: married

One

"We are gathered here today in the face of this company to join together Kimberley Blackstone and Ricardo Perrini in matrimony...."

Jarrod Hammond heard the words of the female marriage celebrant, but his eyes were drawn not to the bride, but to the woman sitting opposite him in the horseshoe circle surrounding his cousin Kim and her soon-to-be husband, Ric Perrini.

Adrenaline kicked in as he leaned back in his chair and let his gaze rake over Briana Davenport, the Australian supermodel who was the face of Blackstone Diamonds. Through the massive yacht's large windows behind her, the late-afternoon sun highlighted the most glorious harbor in the world and created a picture-perfect backdrop for her beauty.

Framed by the Opera House and Sydney Harbour Bridge, and dressed in a silky, pale blue pantsuit that flowed as she moved, she was elegance and sophistication. The epitome of glamour. A crowning glory for the diamond company she symbolized. He could see why Howard Blackstone had chosen her to represent his business.

And just as expensive, Jarrod mused rather cynically, noting with satisfaction the exact moment she saw him looking at her. Her eyelids flickered just a bit before she looked away, but only someone with an internal radar for this woman would pick up on it.

Someone like him.

"If anyone can show just cause—" the celebrant continued.

Much to Jarrod's displeasure, his internal radar was constantly tuned on Briana. It had been that way from the moment he'd set eyes on her at his brother's marriage to her sister four years ago. It had been on high ever since, even though he knew Briana had a serious flaw. An *expensive* serious flaw. She liked money, and plenty of it, and went through it like it was going out of fashion, according to her now-dead sister, Marise.

Of course, being attuned to Briana didn't help when everywhere he turned she was there in front of him: up on billboards...on television...in glossy magazines. Nor was it easy knowing they lived in the same city in another part of the country. Thankfully with her jet-setting around the world as a supermodel, and him with his law practice, Melbourne was big enough for the two of them not to run into each other.

"Ric, do you take Kimberley for your lawful wedded wife, to live in the holy estate of matrimony? Will you love, honor, comfort and..."

But now, seeing Briana in the flesh again—her oh-so-delicious flesh—reminded him why he'd inveigled an invitation to the Blackstone Jewellery launch here in Sydney last Friday and flown up from Melbourne. And why he was glad he'd accepted Kim's invitation today. Being a Hammond at a Blackstone wedding was never going to be easy, but with Briana here, the day suddenly seemed full of sensual possibilities, despite the presence of millionaire Jake Vance, who once again partnered her.

"Kimberley, do you take Ric for your lawful wedded husband, to live in the holy estate of matrimony? Will you love, honor, comfort and..."

Jarrod's mouth tightened as he looked at the man sitting beside Briana. The pair had been photographed together in the Melbourne papers at the St. Valentine's Day races a few weeks ago. And again last Friday at the jewelry launch. Were the two of them lovers? Probably, he decided, not pleased by the burst of irrational jealousy he felt at the thought of her in the other man's bed.

"May this ring be blessed so that he who gives it..." the woman continued.

Dammit, was he being a glutton for punishment by going after her? Hadn't he already made his decision to bed her? A decision based on wanting to find out all he could about her sister for his brother's sake. He'd seen

Matt only two weeks ago and had been shocked at how worn and bitter he'd become. Jarrod and Matt may have been adopted, but they were closer than blood brothers, and he'd do everything in his power to make sure Matt found some inner peace—no matter what it took.

Or whom.

But he couldn't blame his brother for being bitter when his wife, Marise, had died from injuries sustained in a plane crash almost two months ago, along with Howard Blackstone and four others. It had conjured up a myriad of questions: questions that no one had any answers to, except maybe Briana Davenport.

"Wear it as a symbol of love and commitment..."

Surely Briana knew why her sister had been on Howard's plane before it crashed. And she knew if her own sister was having an affair with Howard, the enemy of the Hammond family ever since his greed parted the two family factions many years ago. She just wasn't saying.

And then there'd been the shock of Marise having been named as a beneficiary in Howard's will. A seven-sum figure and the Blackstone jewelry collection was a considerable inheritance for a young mistress. And that begged the question as to whether Blake was really Howard's son and not Matt's. Blake certainly had the same dark hair as Howard, unlike Matt's sandy-blond head. It made Jarrod sick to his stomach to think about it.

"You may now seal the promises you have made with each other with a kiss."

Dammit, the Blackstones had caused enough pain for his family. His parents would be devastated if they found out that Blake was not their grandson, but their great-nephew, instead. Not that it would make any difference to the way they felt about the child. They'd proven that by adopting him and Matt all those years ago. As for Matt and how he would feel about Blake not being his own…

"Ladies and gentlemen, I present to you Mr. and Mrs. Ricardo Perrini."

Just then, as if his angry thoughts had drawn Briana's blue eyes back to him, Jarrod held her gaze among the clapping and the cheers, and let her know with a look what he had decided. She was the woman he wanted.

She was the woman he would have.

While she was waiting to be seated for the wedding feast, Briana sipped champagne and listened with delight as the beaming and slender Jessica Cotter talked about her newly announced pregnancy. They'd spoken last Friday night at the jewelry launch, but it had been a busy night for both of them and their chat had only been brief. Now it was great to be able to catch up with each other.

"Ryan's thrilled," Jessica said, sending the man in question an adoring look across the deck where he stood talking to his just-married sister, Kim.

And the ruthless and handsome Ryan Blackstone smiled back. A warm, love-filled look that was meant for one woman and one woman only—his fiancée.

"You're one very lucky woman, Jess," Briana said with a smile, envious of Jessica's happiness but so very pleased for her.

"I know," Jessica said, grinning. Then her gaze slid to the woman standing next to Ryan, brother and sister clearly both Blackstones. "And doesn't Kim look absolutely gorgeous? That white gown is exquisite, but with her dark hair and green eyes, she looks stunning."

Briana's gaze slid over Kimberley Blackstone, now Kimberley Perrini, who wore an elegant couture wedding dress. "I've got to agree. She's stunning."

"I bet Ric thinks so, too." Jessica gave a dreamy sigh. "This must be so different from the first time they were married in Las Vegas. It just goes to prove that divorce isn't always final."

"I guess it all depends on the couple," Briana said, thinking about some of the people she knew in the modeling world. Her profession wasn't easy on a marriage. She'd seen some wonderful partnerships, as well as some horrors.

"By the way," Jessica said, interrupting her thoughts. "Did you contact Quinn Everard yet about those diamonds Marise left in your safe?"

At the thought of her dead sister, Briana's heart squeezed tight. "Yes, I phoned him the other day. I've been so busy lately that I just kept putting it off. What with work and trying to help Dad cope with Mum's death and now Marise's, it hasn't been a priority."

"That's understandable," Jessica said sympathetically. "You just make sure you take care of yourself, too."

"I will," Briana said, her eyes thanking her friend. "Anyway, Quinn said to drop the diamonds off at his office. He's away at the moment but I can leave them with his office manager. I'll do that tomorrow morning." She grimaced. "Frankly, I'll be glad to know their value so that I can decide what to do with them. Matt said he didn't want anything of Marise's, but I just can't keep them."

Jessica nodded. "Well, Quinn's the man. He's got an excellent reputation as a gem appraiser. He—" All at once her gaze focused on the men across the room and she scowled. "Oh no, I think I'm needed. Ric and Ryan look like they've had enough of each other for a while." She rolled her eyes. "Men!"

Briana chuckled as she watched Jessica hurry away, but she knew that tensions associated with members of the Blackstone family right now weren't anything to laugh about.

Knew it only too well, unfortunately.

Not that any of them held the controversial deaths of her sister and their father against her. They'd all been very considerate. Ric and Ryan had treated her with respect, and Jessica and Kim had become good friends. Not to mention the elegant Sonya Hammond and her charming daughter, Danielle. Though the latter two were not blood relations to Howard Blackstone, they were still related, and they'd shown her kindness at Howard's funeral, and welcomed her warmly today.

Of course, she couldn't think about the Blackstones without thinking about Matt Hammond. Her brother-in-law could be hardnosed but he was also a fine, upstanding man, and hadn't deserved the legacy of doubts her sister had left him and their young son, Blake. His adoptive parents, Katherine and Oliver Hammond, had been wonderful to Marise, too, but her sister hadn't really appreciated them.

As for the older adopted son…it was obvious to her that beneath Jarrod Hammond's veneer of sophistication, he fully believed she and Marise had shared the same liking for the good life that Marise had enjoyed as Matt's wife.

Only, nothing was further from the truth. Marise may have been flighty and always looking for something more, but *she* was happy with her lot in life. And for that she still felt guilty. If only she'd been closer to Marise, maybe then she'd understand why her sister had been keeping company with Howard Blackstone and why he'd left all his jewelry to Marise in his will. But no matter how she'd tried to breach the gap, they were poles apart. She didn't understand how Jarrod couldn't see that.

Just then, her eyes met the man in question across the breadth of the middle deck, and a hush seemed to descend upon everything in the room. An imaginary hush, obviously, though there was nothing imaginary about the hunger in Jarrod Hammond's eyes. The hunger had always been there, waiting…for what, she wasn't sure. He'd certainly made no move to further anything between them over the years.

Not that it would have done him any good. She wasn't getting involved with another high-powered male. Not after Patrick, her ex-business manager and lover, had invested most of her money in a "surefire" deal and had lost it.

No, she didn't need a man in her life.

And definitely not Jarrod Hammond.

Suddenly he started to walk toward her. She wanted to run as fast and as far away as she could, up the stairs and out on the top deck where the breeze off the harbor would cool her heated cheeks, but her strappy high heels seemed fixed to the floor.

And then he was standing in front of her, and she could do nothing but face him and try not to let him overwhelm her with his sheer presence.

"Hello, Briana," he murmured as he leaned in close and kissed her cheek, his firm lips lingering just a whisper too long. "We seem to be running into each other a lot lately."

She tingled. "Yes, we do," she said, then saw his eyes darken at her husky tone. Quickly she cleared her throat, trying not to show that she cared he had touched her. "Um…but I didn't expect to see you here, Jarrod."

"Really?" A cool light came into his eyes. "Why not? Kim is my cousin."

"Yes." And one he must know more than the others, seeing that Kim had worked for the Hammonds until recently.

But that was merely a reason for his presence, not an explanation. The Hammonds and the Blackstones, despite being related, had thrown some pretty wild accusations at each other's dynasties over the years. Marise had once briefly mentioned how Jarrod's father, Oliver, had accused Howard Blackstone of some pretty dastardly things, including marrying Oliver's sister for monetary gain. In retaliation, Howard had accused Oliver of arranging the kidnapping of his two-year-old son, James Blackstone. The child had never been seen again.

"Maybe I'm surprised to see *you* here," Jarrod said, cutting across her thoughts, and she knew nothing much would surprise this man. She had the feeling he'd known she'd be here today.

"Kim and I have been working together on some of the Blackstone events," she said, a touch defensively. "We've become friends."

"Good. She could do with another friend right now."

For a moment, Briana thought he was being sarcastic, but then she realized he was sincere. Something inside her softened. Kim had certainly had it tough these past few months, but coming from him—a Hammond who on his brother's behalf now had another reason to hate any Blackstone—the comment was even more surprising. Perhaps he wasn't as coldhearted as she'd thought?

"She looks beautiful, doesn't she?" Briana said, turning away from him to look at her friend, mainly so she didn't have to look at Jarrod.

"Yes, she does," he said in a seductive voice that made her spin back toward him. He was staring at *her.*

Whatever had softened inside her now turned to mush. She had to force herself not to redden, her years of modeling doing nothing to stop the faint warmth rising up her neck.

She took a sip of champagne, then, "What did you think of the ceremony?" she asked for something to say.

His knowing blue eyes held hers a moment longer before breaking contact. He shrugged. "A wedding's a wedding."

It was such a typical male reaction that she had to

smile. "Really? We're at a lavish affair on a luxury cruiser in the middle of Sydney Harbour on a perfect autumn day, and the daughter of one of Australia's richest men has just re-married her late father's right-hand man." She gave a rueful smile. "No, this wedding isn't just any wedding. This is a *Blackstone* wedding in all its glory."

The corners of his mouth curved with the beginnings of a sexy smile. "Do Blackstones pay you to promote them like this?"

She laughed. "I'd be stupid *not* to promote them, don't you think?"

He paused, his eyes hardening as they swept over her features. "And you're definitely not stupid, are you?"

Her smile disappeared. "That doesn't sound like a compliment."

Something came and went in his eyes. "I admire how far you've come in this business."

She tried not to stiffen, but she did anyway. What was he implying? "It still doesn't sound very flattering," she challenged.

His lips twisted, then he appeared to mentally back off. "So you like to be flattered, do you?"

She realized he'd backed off only because he chose to. "Didn't you know? I need to be flattered at least once every hour," she mocked, then arched a slim eyebrow. "After all, isn't that what all models are about?"

His eyes narrowed slightly, but there was a sardonic tilt to his mouth. "But you're a *super*model."

"So I need to be *super*-flattered," she returned as a waiter offered to refill her half-empty glass of champagne. She put her hand over the glass and shook her head. She didn't need more to drink. She needed her wits about her.

"I'm told I'm usually good at *super*-flattering a woman," Jarrod murmured, once the waiter moved away.

Her gaze flew back to the man beside her and panic stirred in her chest. "I'm sure you are. Usually." In a deliberate movement, she looked around for her date. Where on earth was Jake when she needed him?

And then she saw him listening with mild amusement to Danielle Hammond. The other woman's coppery curls bounced as she moved her head animatedly, her full mouth wide and smiling in a friendly fashion.

"Looks like your date is occupied," Jarrod said pointedly.

She glanced sideways at him and shrugged.

"So you're not the jealous type?"

"Not in the least." She enjoyed Jake's company but, as handsome and charming as he was, he was only a friend. And thankfully he was someone who had nothing to do with the Blackstone dynasty and all its associated problems. But she wasn't about to tell Jarrod any of that. "Danielle's such a sweetie," she added to show her non-jealousy.

"That she is," he agreed slowly, but she could hear in his voice that he was still looking at her, trying to get inside her head and figure her out.

Pretending not to notice, Briana let her gaze wander around the room, forcing herself to concentrate on the other guests. Anything but concentrate on Jarrod Hammond…or let him concentrate on her.

There were about sixty guests and most of the faces were strangers to her, but she did see Sonya Hammond talking to Garth Buick, an urbane and charming man who'd been Howard Blackstone's company secretary. They were only a few feet away and Briana could hear them talking about going sailing together. Something about the way they looked at each other—or perhaps it was the way they were trying *not* to look at each other—made Briana wonder if there was something between the two of them. If so, they were a good match. In her late forties, Sonya had a tall, willowy elegance that complemented the trim and well-toned Garth, who was just a few years older.

"Are you always so trusting?" Jarrod said, bringing her focus back on him.

She'd grimaced. "Unfortunately, no."

His glance sharpened. "What happened to rob you of your trust?"

Heavens, how was she going to get out of this one? She only had to look at that firm jaw to know he wasn't a man to give up when he wanted something.

"Nothing of interest," she said airily, but her heart was pounding in her chest.

"Oh, but I think there is," he said, confirming her suspicions.

"Let it go, Jarrod. It's nothing important." And to prove it, she scooped a canapé off a tray as a waiter passed by.

"Let me be the judge of that."

"Ahh, but I thought you were a property lawyer, not a judge."

His lips began to twitch. "And you're obstructing the course of justice, Briana."

"Or guilty of contempt," she mocked, then popped the canapé into her mouth, feeling pleased with herself.

He laughed out loud, taking her unawares. "I didn't realize you had such a smart mouth."

Because she'd never let him know it before, that's why, she mused, chewing the delicate morsel. She'd never let him get close enough.

So why was she letting him get close now? More importantly, why was he *trying* to get close now, she wondered, watching as his gaze fell to her lips and darkened, as if he were thinking about kissing her. She quickly swallowed, then took another sip of champagne.

Just then, the sound of a helicopter rent through the air as it came close and swooped the yacht. Far too close for Briana's piece of mind.

And obviously for Ric Perrini's.

"Damn the media!" Ric growled, striding across the middle deck to look out the side window of the cruiser right near Briana. "Can't they leave us in peace for one day?"

It broke the moment between her and Jarrod, for which she should have been grateful but wasn't. Instead she kept remembering that gorgeous laugh of his. It sent shivers of desire down her spine.

"I'm already on it," Kim said, coming over to her new husband and slipping her arm inside his. "The captain should be on the phone right now to the water police. They'll sort it out."

"They'd better," Ric warned.

"Anyway, we have more immediate problems. The photographer's about to have chickens if we don't let him take some pictures of us with our guests." She smiled at Briana and Jarrod. "You two will have your photo taken with us, won't you?"

Briana's fingers tightened around her glass. She knew it hadn't been Kim's intention, but even a small mention of her and Jarrod doing something together made her uncomfortable.

"Perhaps later, Kim," Jarrod said with a tight smile, then excused himself and headed to where an older couple stood looking out the back of the cruiser.

There was a flash of disappointment in Kim's eyes and Ric stiffened beside his wife, before she quickly gave his arm a squeeze. For all that Jarrod was here today, it was apparent Kim's falling out with his brother was still an issue between the Hammonds and the Blackstones.

For the Hammonds anyway.

To cover the awkward moment, Briana pasted on her best smile for the new bride. "Hey, that's all the more coverage for me then. You know how I love being in front of the camera."

Kim smiled with gratitude. "Thanks," she murmured, just as the photographer appeared.

Later, when everyone sat down to dinner, Sonya asked Briana how she managed to look so good in front of a camera when it was such hard work.

"You don't know the half of it," Briana said, smiling across the table at the other woman.

"I'd love to hear about it," Sonya said, the warmth in her eyes belying her cool reserve.

Briana obligingly chatted about some of the more obvious facets of modeling, yet she knew they'd all be surprised if she told them the truth. She'd fallen into modeling as a teenager but much preferred being behind the camera than in front of it.

Perhaps one day after she'd made enough money to recoup the money Patrick had lost, she'd further her dream. Until then it really wasn't such a hardship smiling for the camera or showcasing Blackstone jewelry. And it certainly wasn't a hardship attending a Blackstone wedding like this one.

Except for Jarrod.

She groaned inwardly. Lately he was turning up everywhere she went. At the jewelry launch the other night she'd never felt so self-conscious being on show before, but seeing him there in the audience, feeling his eyes upon her, she felt as if she was showcasing *herself,* not the Blackstone jewelry.

And now here he was at the wedding, sitting next to Vincent Blackstone, the late Howard Blackstone's older brother, deep in conversation. From time to time, though, his eyes were on *her.*

"You seem to be pretty cozy with Jarrod Hammond," Jake murmured in her ear, startling her when she must have looked at Jarrod once too often.

Trying to appear nonchalant, she glanced at Jake and

saw a very male look in his eyes that reminded her too much of Jarrod. This guy hadn't missed a thing going on around him. No doubt such ability was part of the reason he was now a rich and successful businessman.

But at least he wasn't the jealous type, she mused. "We're distant in-laws, that's all. Nothing special."

"Really?" he mocked in an arrogant way that said she wasn't fooling him.

"You know, Jake," she said, getting a little irritated being surrounded by males who thought they knew everything. "I think all the testosterone on this boat must be keeping it afloat."

A surprised look entered his eyes then he burst out laughing. For a moment she stared at him, then began to smile in return. It *was* quite funny, now she came to think about it.

"I'd have thought a beautiful woman like yourself would be used to being surrounded by testosterone," Jake teased.

"In the modeling world?" she jokingly scoffed, and received a chuckle from Jake.

"No, I guess not," he agreed with a rueful grin.

Suddenly she caught Jarrod looking at the two of them. A slither went over her skin and quickly she looked away just as the waiter brought the next course. Once the food was served, talk at the table turned to other things.

Briana deliberately didn't look at Jarrod after that, preferring instead to concentrate on the speeches and proceedings, though she was aware of him. Afterward, dark descended and they all moved to the well-lit top deck where the bride and groom began their first dance. Before too long, others had joined them, including her and Jake.

As for Jarrod, he seemed to have disappeared. She remained on edge, at first expecting him to show up at any tick of the clock, but when he didn't, she quickly pushed aside the disappointment that filled her. She wasn't going to let herself be disappointed by a man again, she reminded herself, then promptly did the opposite when she saw the lights from a small boat moving away from the cruiser, taking Jarrod back to shore.

He hadn't even said goodbye, she thought, then something on the shoreline caught her attention. Myriad lights began to flash as the small boat approached them.

The media.

Not that Jarrod would give them a second thought. No doubt he'd stride through the pack to a waiting car like he was parting the Red Sea.

After that the evening seemed flat. Briana smiled and talked, and when it came time for the yacht to return to shore, she was glad that the security people held back the media circus while they made their way into a fleet of cars.

Lights flashed in her eyes as Jake guided her into the back of a limousine, but the media's attention soon focused back on Kim and Ric, who had insisted they would only leave the boat after all their guests had alighted.

"They're a brave couple," Jake said, shaking his head as a shower of flashes seemed to light up the night sky through the back window of the car.

"Yes," Briana agreed. "And very determined to show the world a united front."

His smile disappeared. "I can understand that."

The limousine drove off but they didn't talk much while it weaved through the streets of Sydney to her apartment building. Then Jake walked her to her door.

"I had a good time," he said, moving in closer, pushing a strand of hair off her cheek.

Briana knew it was a prelude to a kiss and she moved in closer, too. Jakc had kissed her before and it had always been nice, but tonight she suddenly wanted him to kiss her like he meant it. As if she was the only woman in the world he wanted.

Only, when the kiss finished, one thing was clear. Jake's kiss had been just a kiss. And by the wry glint in his eye he knew it, too.

"I think you'd better get some sleep," he said, tapping her on the end of her nose with his index finger. And then he pivoted and headed back to the elevator.

Briana watched him go with a sinking feeling in her stomach. Jake was an extremely handsome man who knew how to treat a woman right. And he knew how to kiss. It was just a pity she hadn't felt anything when his lips were on hers. Not like she would if Jarrod Hammond had kissed her.

Of that she was certain.

Two

The next morning Briana caught a taxi to Quinn Everard's office and left the diamonds with his office manager. Then, after another couple of days in Sydney, including lunching with her agent, she caught a plane back to Melbourne on the Wednesday, and drove to her father's house to check on him first. Then she'd go home to her apartment on the other side of the city. She still had to prepare for the Moomba Fashion Show this coming Labor Day weekend at the casino.

So it was mid-afternoon by the time Briana parked in the driveway of the solid brick home that her parents bought when they'd moved to Melbourne from Sydney nearly thirty years ago. They'd never been rich but had been comfortable. Her mother had even insisted on sending her and Marise to one of the top private schools here in Melbourne, after a spinster aunt had left her some money.

Now, when Ray Davenport opened the front door to her, Briana noted with concern that her father was looking tired. He'd been through so much, having kept her mother's secret of the cancer that ravaged her body, until the end, when her mother had become so ill he'd finally told their daughters she was dying.

"Want some coffee, honey?" he asked, walking ahead of her into the kitchen.

"Thanks, Dad. That would be lovely." She followed him, noting the stoop to his shoulders. "By the way, I dropped those diamonds off for an appraisal."

He looked over his shoulder with a frown. "Diamonds?"

"The ones Marise left in my safe."

His face cleared. "Oh, that's right. You found them in your safe after the plane crash, didn't you?"

"Yes." Overcome with grief, she'd nearly forgotten Marise asking for the safe combination to keep some jewelry in there.

Briana had thought nothing of giving the combination to her sister. She'd also let Marise stay in her Sydney apartment once she and her father returned to Melbourne, after Barbara Davenport had been buried next to her own parents in Waverley Cemetery. It was then that Marise seemed to go off the rails, those last few weeks before the plane crash. Their mother's death had devastated Marise, but for her sister to remain in Sydney had been unwarranted.

Especially after she'd started to be seen around town with Howard Blackstone.

Especially when she had a husband and a small son back in New Zealand waiting for her.

No wonder Matt had said he didn't give a damn about any jewelry belonging to Marise. But she knew her brother-in-law wasn't thinking straight, and that was part of the reason she'd decided to get them appraised. Perhaps if they were valuable they'd be worth keeping for Blake as a memento of his mother. Or maybe one day Matt would forgive his late wife and want the diamonds back. In the meantime, getting the diamonds valued was something *she* could do for her dead sister.

"So you're getting them appraised, you say?" her father said now, bringing her back to the moment. Again she noticed he didn't look well.

She stood in the kitchen doorway, her forehead creasing. "Dad, are you okay?"

A moment crept by.

"Dad?"

He looked up at her then, and there was a despairing look in his eyes that had her sucking in a sharp breath. "I'm a thief, Briana. I've stolen some money."

The breath caught in her lungs. "Wh-what?"

"I stole from Howard Blackstone."

She stared in astonishment. "My God! How much?"

He paused, then let out a shaky sigh. "One million dollars."

* * *

Briana was still reeling from her father's confession as she sat at the roulette table at the casino on Saturday evening. It had taken such an effort to keep her mind on the fashion show today, then again at the cocktail party this evening, but somehow she'd put a professional smile on her face. Afterward, not ready to go home to an empty apartment, she had stayed on.

It wasn't every week a daughter learned her father had stolen a million dollars. And from a "secret" account he'd been told about while working as an accountant for one of Australia's richest men thirty years ago, after Howard's previous accountant had passed on that bit of information.

Nor was the reason her father had taken the money in the first place enough to stop Ray Davenport from going to jail. Medical expenses for his wife's cancer, then a world cruise after a terminal diagnosis would garner immense sympathy, but in the end, the law would not condone embezzlement.

A lump wedged in her throat. With the newspapers continuing to report on the anonymous buy-up of Blackstone shares, she could just imagine how the media would hound her poor father, not to mention herself. They'd already gone through that after the plane crash. She didn't want to go through it again.

Besides, it wouldn't look good that her father had never forgiven Howard for firing Barbara when she'd become pregnant with Marise. Yet even after the Davenports had pulled up roots and moved from Sydney to

Melbourne, the Blackstones had ended up an intrinsic part of their lives. In the latter years, Marise had worked for Blackstone Diamonds in sales and marketing, then Briana had found herself a model and the face of Blackstone Diamonds. And then Marise had been with Howard on the flight to New Zealand, and had died in the aftermath of the crash. It was crazy, but it was as if destiny had somehow wanted the Davenports and the Blackstones to keep a connection.

And how ironic that his supermodel daughter couldn't help Ray out with money when he needed it. Her new million-dollar contract with Blackstone's was due to be renewed in three months' time, but nothing was ever certain until it was signed. Until then she had just enough to live on, thanks to her ex-business manager and lover, Patrick, who had convinced her to invest nearly all her money in an unbuilt apartment complex. It had sounded like a good investment at the time, until the developers had gone bust and she'd lost the lot.

She'd never told her parents about it, feeling like a sucker. They'd known she'd invested her money. They just hadn't known she'd lost it.

All at once someone sat down on the seat beside her, and the hairs on the back of her neck stood up. She turned toward the man who suddenly and completely filled her vision.

"Jarrod!"

"Briana," he murmured, his blue eyes trapping hers for a heart-stopping second.

She moistened her mouth even as she realized something. "You knew I'd be here, didn't you?"

One brow rose. "Did I?"

"It's too much of a coincidence otherwise," she said, letting him know she wasn't being hoodwinked.

He shrugged. "Perhaps."

Her forehead creased. "You want to see me?"

"Oh yes," he drawled, his gaze going over her long, blond wavy hair that tumbled around her head, before dipping to the creamy expanse of her neck and shoulders above the black cocktail dress, then further down and over the gathered bust held together by a diamond center clasp.

Her heart dropped to her toes but she managed a glare. "I meant that you wanted to *talk* to me?" she said, in no frame of mind to fend off his seduction.

He paused, his face turning unreadable now. "Yes."

She waited for him to speak, and when he didn't, she said, "Then talk."

"Not here." He got to his feet, his hand cupping her bare elbow, sending a warming shiver through her. "Come have a drink with me in the lounge."

She looked up at him standing so close beside her, an air of command exuding from him, threatening to engulf her. She wanted to say no, but couldn't think up a suitable excuse. "Just for a moment."

Then she stood up too and his eyes approved the short, glamorous dress. Heat curled in her stomach, before he led her away from the crowds and into one of the lounges. It was quieter in here with plenty of small tables circled by large comfortable leather chairs.

He took her to some seats in a secluded corner that was much too intimate for Briana's peace of mind, but when she saw some of the other patrons looking their way she was rather thankful no one could listen in on their conversation.

A waiter immediately came over to them, and she agreed to join Jarrod in a brandy. It would calm her nerves, she decided, watching him place their order, his self-confidence and sophistication an attraction many women would find appealing.

Dressed in dark trousers and a sports blazer with a white T-shirt underneath, he could have been a male model himself if there hadn't been such a hard edge to him. Those blue eyes clearly showed that hardness, an arrogance that would never let anyone dictate to him, let alone a camera.

"No Jake Vance today?" he said once the waiter left.

"I gave him the day off," she quipped.

The edges of that firm, sensual mouth tilted. "I doubt Jake would think of it that way."

She doubted it, too, but she didn't say so.

His smile disappeared and he fixed her with a candid gaze. "You and Jake are an item then?"

She lifted her chin. "I don't think that's any of your business."

He considered her for a moment, a pulse beating in his cheekbone. "The two of you were having a good laugh together at Kim's wedding."

For a moment she didn't know what he was talking

about. Then she remembered her comment about testosterone keeping the boat afloat and a bubble of laughter rose in her throat.

His eyes narrowed. "So there *is* something going on between you two."

She lost her amusement, not sure why he was being so insistent. "You wanted to talk," she reminded him, crossing her legs, pretending this line of questioning wasn't getting to her.

His eyes plunged to her legs in the ultrasheer silk stockings revealed by the ruffled hem, admired them, then rose back up to her face. "Are the two of you lovers?"

Her own eyes widened in dismay. "I don't believe I'm hearing this."

He held her gaze. "Tell me the truth, Briana."

Panic stirred in her chest but she kept it at bay. "Why, Jarrod? Why do you want to know about Jake and me?"

"Because if he doesn't want you, *I* do."

Her head reeled back. "What?"

"I want you to be my lover," he repeated firmly, leaving no doubt this time.

She gave him a glance of utter disbelief. "You can't be serious!"

"You deny you want me, too?"

She swallowed past her suddenly dry throat, tried to speak and had to swallow again. "I *can* deny it and I do," she lied, knowing she couldn't admit wanting him. It would give him an unfair advantage over her. One he wouldn't hesitate to use.

"Why sound so shocked? I'd have thought a woman

like yourself—" he gave a tiny pause "—would be used to such propositions."

Her blood pressure began to rise. "You mean because I'm a model?"

He inclined his dark head. "What other reason would there be?" he said silkily, as the waiter arrived with their brandy.

Her lips flattened with anger. At the wedding, Jarrod had made a similar comment about how far she'd come in the business. It hadn't sounded like a compliment back then, and neither did this comment. Had he thought she'd slept her way to the top? It sickened her to think that, yet why she cared she didn't know. It would serve him right if she called his bluff.

Why not?

"Okay, I'll sleep with you," she said, once the waiter left. "For a million dollars."

His eyes flickered then became shuttered. "That can be arranged."

Her brain stumbled. "What?"

He shot her a dry look. "Sleep with me and I'll give you a million dollars."

He'd well and truly called her bluff. "But—but you don't have that kind of money to give away."

His brows lifted. "You know that for a fact, do you?"

Oh heavens. Was she stupid or what? Apart from coming from a wealthy family, he'd made a name for himself as a property lawyer. Of course he'd have a million dollars to spare. What an idiot she was!

From somewhere she managed to scoff, "Ill-gotten gains, Jarrod?"

Contempt flashed in his eyes. "No. I'll leave that to the Blackstones."

"That's my employer you're talking about," she said coolly.

"Doesn't change a thing. The Blackstones are far from saints." He picked up the two glasses and passed one to her. "Now, about our agreement—"

She took the brandy glass from him, but an acute sense of panic raced through her again. "Keep your money. I don't want it. I—" She stopped.

She *did* need the money.

Needed it more than he could ever know.

"Having second thoughts?" he asked.

"No." She took a sip of brandy, and wished her denial carried the same strength as the alcohol now burning her throat.

"We can always do with more money," he pointed out, watching her as if knowing all along it would come back to this.

This being money.

Of course, she now realized that by even suggesting the million dollars she was playing into his belief that she was cut from the same cloth as her sister. Marise had said she'd fallen in love with Matt, but Briana suspected Matt's wealth hadn't hurt, either. And then there was Marise and Howard....

"A million dollars, Briana," he reminded her.

No, she couldn't do it. She wasn't for sale.

Then she forced her heart to steady itself. What if she looked upon it as a loan, asked a small voice inside her. A loan she would pay back once her contract with Blackstones was renewed.

A million-dollar contract.

But if it wasn't renewed? What if they got someone else to replace her as the face of Blackstone Diamonds?

What if—

No, she wouldn't think about "what if's". Nor would she think about not repaying the money to him at all. It just wasn't in her to be underhanded.

But could she make love to Jarrod Hammond?

Oh God. How much of a hardship would that really be? She was attracted to him, no doubt about it. Intensely attracted, if she were to be honest with herself. It wasn't like she would be making a huge sacrifice and giving her body to someone who was revolting and wouldn't appreciate her. Jarrod would definitely appreciate her. Oh yes. She didn't know a man who would appreciate her better.

"Briana?"

She glanced at him then. He looked cool and calm, yet she sensed he was anything but. He wanted her just as much as she wanted him. So what harm would she do in sleeping with him? It wasn't as though she would be doing anything against her will.

On the contrary…

"It's a deal," she heard herself say.

He scowled. "It is?"

"You don't have the money?" she said with a rush of

disappointment that was about more than just getting her father out of trouble.

His dark brows straightened. “I have it.” Just as quickly a considering light came into his eyes. “But now that I think of it,” he drawled, “a million dollars for one night *is* a bit too much money—even for the face of Blackstone's.”

Her lips tightened. He'd been playing with her. “Fine. That's it then.”

“No, I'd say it's worth a month of nights together, don't you?”

She stiffened in shock. “No! I can't. A month is too long.”

He shrugged his broad shoulders. “That's my offer. Become my mistress for one month and I'll give you a million dollars.”

She swallowed hard. “That wasn't what I agreed to, Jarrod, and you know it.”

“You agreed to sleep with me. True. But we didn't mention a timeframe.”

She shook her head, not understanding him. “Why can't you be satisfied with one night?”

He didn't move a muscle. “Can you?”

She winced inwardly. Could she do it for one whole month? One night was so different. Or was it? Wouldn't only one night make her feel as if she really were selling herself? Wouldn't being his mistress for a month make her feel better about it all? Or was she just kidding herself?

“Briana, you want the money. Don't deny it.” He waited a moment. “And I want you.”

She cleared her throat and ignored an inward shudder of heat that couldn't be attributed to the brandy. "Who said I want the money?" she asked, trying to put him off the scent of her father's trail.

"You don't? Then it must be *me* you want," he mocked, his smirk saying he'd backed her into a corner.

Mentally kicking herself, she raised her chin. "I'm not denying the money wouldn't come in handy." She saw the hard look that entered his eyes. "And I don't deny that sleeping with a man such as yourself wouldn't be a—nice experience."

He smiled sardonically. "I'm glad you think so."

"But a month does seem a bit too long."

He swirled the brandy in his glass, then looked up at her. "Take it or leave it. But let me tell you, if you leave it, there won't be another chance."

Suddenly a feminine power settled over her, giving her confidence. "You might want to rethink that, Jarrod. After all, I've got something you want—my body. And if in a month's time I say I want you, I'm pretty sure I won't have to beg."

His nod acknowledged her words. "Oh, I don't deny that. But next time there won't be any money involved, sweetheart. It'll be just you and me. I won't be offering a million dollars again."

She gritted her teeth. He was a clever devil. Somehow he sensed she wouldn't walk away from the money. What he didn't know was that she *couldn't* walk away from it. Not if she wanted to help save her father.

So what if she accepted Jarrod's extended offer? The month would go fast. She had quite a few modeling engagements around the country to give her a break from Jarrod's overwhelming presence. At least there was that.

And perhaps she could even prove to him that she *wasn't* like her sister, she thought, then immediately rebuked herself. Why would she even want to? She owed Jarrod Hammond nothing.

She placed her glass of brandy on the coffee table in front of her. "I'll give you until the end of the month. That's three weeks. Take it or leave it," she said, putting the ball back into his court.

A moment crept by.

Static crackled the air between them.

Then he drained his glass and put it down next to hers. "I'll book a room," he said, about to get to his feet.

Her eyes widened. "What? Here?"

He stopped with a frown. "I thought it might be easier for our first night together."

"For whom?"

"You." He watched her in silence for a moment. "If you like, we can go back to my apartment…or to yours."

That was the last thing she wanted. "No," she said quickly. "A room here will be fine."

"Good." He stood up. "Wait here. I'll send you a note to say what suite I'll be in." He glanced around at the other patrons, then back at her. "I'm sure you don't want your reputation to suffer if somebody sees us going up together."

"Not to mention yours," she managed to say, still reeling from what tonight's outcome would be.

His eyes darkened. "I don't give a damn about my reputation, Briana. It might be wise to remember that." He strode off.

Three

It was silly to feel so nervous, Briana told herself as she tapped lightly on the door to the room fifteen minutes later. Heavens, she'd paraded in front of prime ministers and heads of state, done photo shoots in the middle of huge crowds, stood practically naked backstage at fashion shows, yet nothing made her feel as exposed as she did right now.

And was it any wonder, she decided when Jarrod opened the door to the deluxe suite and she met the full power of those intense blue eyes. Her stomach did a slow somersault.

And just as slowly, he reached out and curled his hand around her wrist, drawing her into the room before closing the door behind them. There he stood looking down at her, his hand still holding her, his palm warmly touching her skin, his thumb resting against the tender inside of her wrist where her pulse raced. She could feel him through every living cell in her body.

And then his gaze dropped to her mouth. He was going to kiss her. She could even feel herself lean just the barest hint toward him. Suddenly she wanted those lips on hers…wanted that body against hers.

"Have you eaten?"

His words snapped her out of her trance. Dismayed at how easily she would have succumbed, she stepped back, letting his hand drop away from her. "Just some finger food at the cocktail party," she said, walking casually into the suite. A wall of floor-to-ceiling glass drew her attention to the city lights below, but Briana only gave the view a quick glance. The world was out there but tonight that's where it would stay.

"You look disappointed a moment ago."

Her heart slammed against her ribs as she glanced across at him. "I did?" She shrugged. "I thought—"

"That I wouldn't waste any time getting you into bed?" A seductive glint entered his eyes. "Briana, being in your company, looking at you, isn't wasting time. Far from it." A smile touched his lips. "The ravishing comes later."

Her breath quickened. He made it sound so… ravishing! "Yes—well—"

"Unless you'd like me to start now instead of ordering you some food?" he drawled.

She sent him a wry look. "No thanks. I'd prefer soup."

His lips twitched. And then his gaze swept over her and awareness danced between them again, and for a moment she thought he really was going to come over to her and ravish her on the spot. And she wanted him to. Dear Lord, she did.

He broke eye contact and strode toward the phone. "I'll order room service," he said, his voice sounding gruff.

Knowing she had affected him, her heart skipped a beat. "I'll just go and freshen up."

He indicated across the width of the room. "The bedroom's that way."

The bedroom.

Carrying her small purse, she took her time to walk across the room, while fighting every instinct to break into a run and lock the door behind her like some frightened virgin. Wouldn't that go down well, she mused with a dash of humor.

The problem was that's exactly how she felt. This was her first time with Jarrod and she was feeling overwhelmed. Despite knowing him for years, despite now acknowledging to herself that she had wanted him for years, there was a difference in the *doing.* A huge difference. She doubted she could ever have prepared herself for this.

Needless to say, seducing women was par for the course for him. He would have done all this before. He certainly seemed to know his way about the suite. He'd probably even met some other women here, just like he'd met her tonight. Had he brought them up here, too?

No, she wasn't going to think about that. She had enough to worry about tonight, she decided as she entered the lavish bedroom, her eyes immediately fastening on the huge bed and her heartbeat skidding to a screeching stop. She and Jarrod would make love on that bed tonight. The thought made her go weak at the knees.

She hurried into the equally giant bathroom and freshened her lipstick. Then she combed through her wavy tresses that bounced along her shoulders as she moved, though why she bothered she wasn't sure. Jarrod would only mess her hair up, just like he would mess with her dress and…

Help!

She took some deep breaths. Okay, so she could stay in here and act like a coward, or she could go out there and face the music. She'd made a deal with the devil, but that deal still stood. And unfortunately so did the devil.

She didn't stay in there long. There was no reason to hide from him or their situation, though she had a few things to say to him first.

"I hope I can count on you not to tell anyone about this," she said, once back in the main area, her chin held high.

He scowled as he stepped away from the bar, carrying two glasses of wine. "Why would I? What we do is our own business."

"As long as we're clear on that."

He handed her a glass and gestured for her to sit on the sofa. "I'm a grown man, not some high-school kid. I don't need to prove anything by telling the world."

She sank down on the soft leather lounge and hoped she could believe him. Patrick had been different, a fact she'd only found out after she'd ended their affair. Apparently he'd often boasted about bedding the face of

Blackstone's. She wished Jarrod was the same type, then she might have the strength to leave right now, but she instinctively knew he wasn't.

He sat down on the chair opposite. "But first, tell me why."

Her throat almost closed up, knowing instantly what he meant. "Er…why?"

His eyes said she wasn't deceiving him. "Why you're willing to sleep with me now and not in the last four years."

She took a sip of her wine before answering. "You never asked before."

And she knew the reason for it. He considered her the same as Marise and hadn't wanted a bar of her. She knew that, and had felt protected by it. Until today.

"Oh, I wanted to ask. But you knew that, didn't you? There's always been an attraction between us."

Her mouth went dry. "You're imagining things."

"The only thing I'm imagining is you in bed with me. And soon I won't need my imagination for that."

Her breath suspended for a full five seconds.

His eyes held hers captive. "Why now, Briana?"

She slowly released her breath and pasted on a cynical smile. "How can I refuse a million dollars *and* the chance to have sex with a man like you?"

He sent her a measured look. "Don't try and pick a fight by insulting me. You're here of your own free will. If you don't want to go through with it, then say so now." A heartbeat passed. "I want you with every breath I take, but I won't force you."

Her heart bumped against her ribs. Oh, how she

wished she could blame him for all this. But he was right. She'd made the choice to be here tonight, if only for her father's sake.

"It won't be force," she agreed, then saw him visibly relax, but he kept his eyes trained on her.

"Tonight is the beginning of our three weeks together, Briana. Nothing more. Are you clear about that?"

Her body immediately tensed. "Very clear. And by the way, *you* were the one who wanted the full month together," she reminded him. Oh, how she'd love to tell him where to shove his money.

"I'm not talking about a month. I'm talking about anything beyond that. I'm not after a long-term relationship."

She gave a derisive snort. "Long-term relationship? With you? I'd rather put my head in an oven."

His hard sensual mouth lifted at the corners. "Now, that would be such a waste."

"Not from where I'm sitting."

He gave a light chuckle as someone knocked lightly on the door and called out, "Room service."

Jarrod pushed himself to his feet and went to let the waiter in. Briana got a good look at the cut of his tailored trousers and blazer from behind. Superb. And so was the masculine body beneath it, she grudgingly admitted, even as she realized something else.

"Wait!" she hissed just as he went to open the door. She jumped up and almost ran across the room to the bedroom and out of sight. She didn't want anyone seeing her there.

A couple of minutes later, Jarrod called to her, "You can come out now."

Feeling slightly foolish, she straightened her shoulders and calmly walked back into the living area, constantly aware of his eyes on her every movement, and trying to keep her own eyes off him. He'd taken off the blazer, and the white T-shirt underneath exposed the muscles of his upper torso.

"Ashamed to be seen with me?" he mocked, holding out a chair for her at the small dining table.

She shrugged. "Don't take it personally. I'd do the same with any man."

His eyes hardened. "Is that so?"

She ignored the implication in his eyes and sat on the offered chair. "Don't you know? The media would love to catch me in a compromising situation such as this."

He walked around the table and sat opposite her. "I'd have thought you'd revel in media attention," he said, showing his low opinion of her.

She flinched inwardly but on the outside, she arched a brow. "You really think I would welcome bad publicity?"

"No, I guess not," he admitted, and she felt the tightness inside her unwind a little. "No doubt bad publicity wouldn't look too good for the face of Blackstone's," he said, lifting the lid off his plate of food.

Briana felt the words sting.

Then he looked up and caught her staring at him. "Aren't you going to eat?"

She shook her head.

He watched her with an observant eye. "Are you okay?"

Suddenly it all got the better of her. "Okay?" she choked, throwing her napkin aside. "I'm about to make love with a stranger, Jarrod. Is it any wonder I'm on edge?"

"I'm not a stranger, Briana," he corrected calmly.

"For all intents and purposes, you are." Unable to sit still a moment longer, and knowing she couldn't eat now anyway, she walked over to the windows. "Can we please get this over and done with?"

Silence hung in the air behind her.

"Don't sound so eager," he drawled, but a moment later she heard movement. "Let's have some privacy, shall we?"

Tension rattled inside her as the suite flooded in darkness, leaving only a faint glow from the city lights beyond the glass. She still didn't turn around. She needed to focus on those city lights, to remember she was here for a purpose.

"Will you respect me in the morning, Jarrod?" She heard herself mutter the cliché, but needed to say it all the same.

"Yes," he said quietly, close behind her, so close his breath stirred strands of her hair. "But will *you* respect you in the morning?"

She thought about that, surprised by his astuteness. His question had dispelled any hint she was selling herself, and she was grateful to him for that. "Yes," she murmured.

And then his hands cupped her bare shoulders, the thin straps of her dress were little protection against him. "I'll make this special for you, Briana."

She could see his reflection as if they were standing in

front of a mirror, the gleam in his eyes seeming to pierce the glass to reach her, seeming to suspend them in time.

Her throat thickened. "I know."

All at once he slid his hand under her golden-blond hair, held it up as if loving the feel of it, then letting it fall like sparkling champagne over her shoulders.

"You're stunning," he murmured, admiration in his voice as he pushed some strands aside to kiss her nape in a gesture that was simply and deliciously sensuous. "A natural beauty."

For a split second she tried to stay in control…tried but soon weakened when his kisses continued to caress her skin. She lowered her lashes, silently shocked at how easy she was succumbing to his touch.

Yet it wasn't just this moment between them. Jarrod was right about there having always been an attraction between them. And that attraction had been unrelenting in its pursuit of them. Tonight, right now, was the culmination of it all.

She couldn't help herself. She tilted her head to the side to allow him easier access—and she gave in. There was no going back now. Nor did she want to. She wanted to be in his arms.

Slowly he undid the zipper at the back of her dress, his lips whispers of sensation as they followed the lowering zipper, making their way down her spine, kissing her where no man had ever kissed before. It was a seduction of the senses that made her head spin.

At the base of her spine he let go of the zipper, and her dress plummeted to the floor and pooled around her ankles. She held her breath, frozen in this instant, watching in the glass as he straightened behind her, all the while admiring her lacy black bra, matching high-cut panties and thigh-high silk stockings.

"My very own model." His hands splayed over her hips as he moved closer, letting her feel his arousal.

A moan escaped her but she managed to say, "Supermodel," and was proud of herself for still having some sort of fight left in her.

He gave a husky chuckle, then lowered his head. He placed his lips against her shoulder and began to nibble at even more pleasure points she never knew she had. When his hands slid around to capture her lace-covered breasts and his fingers lightly squeezed her nipples with the sweetest torment, she moaned with wanting him.

"Too much?" he muttered.

"Yes."

"Good."

He scooped her up and carried her into the bedroom, spreading her across the thick bedspread as if she were a pleasure to be savored. She lay there in the lamplight and stared up at him. His eyes glittered as he took in her half-naked state, her breasts eagerly straining against the lace, the V-shape of her high-cut panties a sensual delight.

His gaze soaked her up, then landed on her face. "Do you realize I've never kissed you?" he muttered roughly, his eyes focusing on her mouth.

She inadvertently moistened her lips. "Same here."

Neither of them smiled. The moment was too intense.

He pulled the T-shirt over his head, his chest bronzed

and sprinkled with hair. He kicked off his shoes and slid onto the bed next to her. And then he claimed her mouth in a kiss that was so passionate it made her head spin. This first touch of his firm lips against her softer ones was more than she had ever expected, more than she'd ever wanted from a man—until now.

And then his tongue parted her lips and stole into her mouth, stole the breath from her, demanding she give him everything of herself. When she capitulated, his groan of appreciation sent a thrill through her as she clung to him like there was no tomorrow.

Right now there *was* no tomorrow. There was only him and her, and the wonderful sensations he was stirring inside her. He undid her bra and eased back, the lace falling away, and she quivered when his fingertips brushed her bare breasts.

"Aah, something else that needs kissing," he murmured as he lowered his head and took a nipple in his mouth, playing with it with his tongue, then sucking in the sweetest of tortures.

Needing to touch him, to be a partner in this, her hands cupped the back of his head and held him to her. She loved spreading her fingers through the short hair, loved it even better when she slipped her hands down to his sculpted shoulders, then the length of his back to the waistband of his trousers.

He shuddered and muttered low in his throat, "You're distracting me." Then he took a deep breath and got to his knees beside her. "Now, what else needs my attention?" he teased, though his eyes were dark with desire as his palm glided down over her stomach, farther down where he dallied and stroked her through her panties, until heat washed over her and made her limbs tremble.

And then his gaze dropped to those trembling limbs, covered by the sheer silk stockings. "I love these things on you," he rasped, slipping his finger under the band of one stocking, and ever so slowly peeling it down her smooth leg. His lips followed the trail until she breathed his name through parted lips.

He repeated the process with the other leg, and when she breathed his name again, his lips trailed back up to her thighs, up the center of her panties where he paused to inhale her.

He turned his head and looked up at her. "Are you sure?"

Tender warmth entered her heart. He was giving her another chance to back out, another chance to say no to all this. As if she could now.

"Yes, I'm sure," she said on a whisper, and that was all the encouragement he needed.

He rolled off the bed and shed the rest of his clothes, and he was suddenly, magnificently, naked. She stared at his unashamed erection, the hardness of him, the powerful male perfection, and she knew that she had to have him inside her. She put out her hand to reach for him, then stopped.

Instead, she lifted her bottom off the bed, pushing her panties down and off herself. Her eyes connected with his as she held them in the air with one finger before dropping them on the floor like a flag of surrender. It was a surrender she willingly made tonight. There was no tomorrow after all.

Something smoldered in the depths of his eyes, and a pulse leaped along his jaw, making her hold her breath. A moment later, he didn't say a word as he reached for the condom from the bedside table and sheathed himself, before coming back to her, kissing her deeply, the full length of his body pressing her down against the mattress.

She kissed him back, loving the feel of his hair-roughened chest against her own tender breasts, the heat of his arousal as he melded into her femininity, filling her completely. She felt like she had never made love before. Not like this.

And then he stopped kissing her, and his eyes captured hers with a look that was undeniably male. It was a triumphant look that said he was here, he had conquered and now he would take.

She thrilled to the silent communication, allowing him his moment of masculinity. And then he began to move his body inside her with long, slow strokes that had her own body raising to meet him with a feminine power of her own. Together they built pleasure upon pleasure, until slow was no longer enough, and fast and deep became a necessity, an essential part of their love-making. Of them.

And together they came as one.

If any woman in the world had been worth a million dollars, it was the woman next to him, Jarrod reflected the next morning as he lay facing Briana sleeping on the pillow next to him. They'd made love three times throughout the night. Three times and he still hadn't had enough of her.

She was dazzling, this golden glamour girl with her velvet eyelashes fanning her smooth cheeks, and her blond hair tousled so sexily over her naked shoulders. The sweet scent of her gorgeous body drifted up beneath the sheet and reeled him in, making the blood pulse in his temples, rush through his body.

Suddenly he wanted her a fourth time.

And a fifth.

And he would have her, too.

Just not right now, he thought regretfully as he glanced at the clock and saw the time. Dammit. He had a meeting with a client in an hour. A very important one, or he would cancel it. But the guy was going overseas later today, and needed a Sunday morning appointment.

Sighing with regret, he slid his hand off Briana's slim hip. It was probably for the best anyway. Despite his body's urges, he needed a moment to himself. Why, he wasn't sure, except that having Briana in his arms had been fulfilling in a way he'd never felt before. And that just didn't make sense. Why did he have to feel this way about a woman beautiful enough and sexy enough to eat?

Yet it was more than a physical sexiness. It was something in her. Something that drew him to her. Drew many men, no doubt, he thought as cynicism gnawed at his gut. How many lovers had seen her like this? Probably too many to count. She may have put on an act about accepting the money, but she'd still accepted his offer.

She was definitely a gold-digger, even if something wasn't quite right here. His lawyer's instincts told him there was more to her taking the money than she was letting on. But what?

His dark brows knitted together. Perhaps he just wanted to believe she had a motive that wasn't attached to the money. More fool him. In his experience, beautiful women couldn't be trusted. They'd always wanted something, always had an angle. The only exception was his adopted mother, Katherine Hammond. She was lovely inside and out.

But his birth mother, an ice-cold beauty whose looks had started to wear thin, was out for all she could get. She'd given him up for adoption to remain footloose and fancy-free. She'd told him so the first time she'd come looking for a handout. The times he'd seen her since hadn't changed his mind.

She and Briana would get on well.

Or would they, he wondered, his eyes resting on Briana, her sheer beauty making him doubt himself. But he had to remember she was the sister of his dead sister-in-law. She and Marise were the same breed of women. Out for all they could get. Marise had proved it with his brother. Briana had just proven it with him.

He slipped out of bed and reached for his checkbook, wrote out the million-dollar check and put it on the pillow he'd just vacated. Then he left Sleeping Beauty in the bedroom, closing the door behind him to go into the main suite to make a phone call. Soon he'd head home to shower and change before his meeting.

But as he hung up the phone, he heard a noise in the bedroom. He strode over and opened the door, but she must not have heard him. She was sitting up in bed, having wrapped the sheet around herself. In her hands was the check and she was looking down at it as if she was defeated rather than pleased.

Something twisted inside his gut, reminding him that there was more to this than met the eye. "Isn't that what you wanted, Briana?"

Her head shot up, her wide-eyed beauty latching on to him. "I thought you'd left," she accused, heat rushing into her cheeks.

Her reaction wasn't what he'd expected from such a woman of the world. For a moment she almost looked…guileless.

"You mean, you were *hoping* I'd left," he said, leaning against the doorjamb, fascinated by every aspect of her. What was going on in that mind of hers?

She angled a chin that was more defiant than delicate right now. "So you don't feel you got value for the money, Jarrod?"

"You know I did. And it's not over yet. We have three weeks of—getting to know each other."

Her lips briefly stretched in a fake smile, then not. "How nice."

"Yes, just like your 'nice' experience last night," he drawled, reminding her of her words last night down in the casino lounge. *Nice* didn't describe the half of it. "At least, I assume it was as 'nice' for you as it was for me."

"Searching for compliments, Jarrod?"

All at once he'd had enough. As much as he liked verbally sparring with her, he had other things to do this morning. "What do you have planned for the rest of the long-weekend?"

She blinked, then wariness clouded her eyes. "Why?"

"I want you to spend it with me."

"So soon?" she said with obvious dismay.

His mouth twisted. "Your enthusiasm is refreshing. Is that a problem?"

She took a ragged breath. "I guess not."

His mouth flattened in a grim line. Anyone would think he'd asked her to give up all her earthly possessions. "Do you have any further engagements this weekend?"

She shook her head. "No, just some things to do in the lead-up to the Grand Prix next weekend."

Yes, the papers were already advertising her attendance at the Melbourne Grand Prix. "Look, I've got an appointment with a client, but I'll be back in a couple of hours to take you to lunch. And tomorrow we can go to the Moomba Festival together."

"Oh, but—"

"I've asked them to send you up some new clothes to gad about in now," he said, preempting her.

Anger flared in her eyes. "I don't want a new set of clothes to gad about in."

"Then wear none," he mocked.

Her mouth thinned. "I prefer my own clothes, thank you."

He glanced at his watch then back at her. Time was running out. "Just relax, order some breakfast and take another nap. You didn't get much sleep last night. I'll be back at noon."

"And if I don't want to spend any more time with you?"

"Then I'll know you're not a woman of your word." He turned and walked out of the hotel room.

Four

After Jarrod left the suite, Briana wasn't sure how long she sat in the king-size bed, cursing him, cursing herself for being attracted to such a man. He'd made love to her last night as if she'd been meant to be in his arms all along. He'd made her feel special and complete, taken her to heights she'd never imagined. She could still feel the remnants of his lovemaking; her breasts were still tender from his touch, her mouth still swollen from his kisses, her lower body still sensitive from his possession.

And she *had* been possessed, there was no doubt about it. Possessed by him. Possessed by her desire for him.

The latter had been a shock.

She couldn't remember even coming close to this with Patrick. No, Patrick had taken what he'd wanted, when he'd wanted in bed, but had never really given her the same fulfillment. Because she'd been in love with him, she hadn't let herself think about it. Her love had covered up a multitude of his flaws…until her rose-colored glasses had been well and truly ripped off her.

And now Jarrod Hammond was making her feel special again, not because she'd fallen in love with him, but because he treated her as the woman he wanted.

She didn't fool herself that it was more than sex—for either of them. He'd wanted to possess her body and he had. She'd wanted him to make love to her, and that was the reason she was feeling fulfilled. Nothing more. It was only about sex. Good sex, admittedly.

All paid for and delivered, she reminded herself, making a half-choked sound as she looked down at the check in her hands. She still couldn't believe she'd given her body to a man for a million dollars. Her father would be horrified. *She* was horrified.

Yet, to be honest, Jarrod hadn't made her feel as if she'd sold her body to him. And that was totally crazy. Any other man would have made her feel cheap.

What was she going to tell her father about the money she'd suddenly acquired? She'd found it lying around in an old bank account? No, too far-fetched. Only Howard Blackstone had kept money in old, "secret" accounts, she mused cynically.

Then the answer came to her. The check was one of Jarrod's, so she would tell her father she'd asked Jarrod for a loan to buy more property. Yes, that was it! Her father probably wouldn't think anything out of the ordinary, not with Jarrod being a Hammond, and with Marise being married to Jarrod's brother.

Of course, loan or not, she still had to pay the money back. She just hoped to high heaven that Blackstone Diamonds wanted to continue their contract with her.

And if she couldn't pay it back? No, she wouldn't think about being beholden to Jarrod any longer than necessary. As it was, he had started to boss her around already, telling her to stay in bed and take a nap, buying her clothes, telling her to wait in the room until he got back, expecting she'd go to lunch with him.

Did that mean he expected her to do everything he asked? Would he expect her to be at his beck and call for the next three weeks?

She was no man's plaything. Not even for a million dollars, she told herself as she pushed aside a sense of trepidation and asked herself what to do next. Oh, she'd keep her word to spend the next three weeks with him, and she'd no doubt enjoy some of it. But she wasn't about to wait around this hotel room for him to return. If he wanted to take her to lunch, then she'd leave him a note and go home to her apartment until he called. She certainly wasn't chasing him. If necessary, she'd meet him at the restaurant.

And she would still be a woman of her word, she decided, throwing back the sheet and pushing her naked body out of bed.

Of course, as soon as her doorbell buzzed, Briana knew who it would be. Despite having a doorman who was harder to get past than a crocodile, somehow Jarrod had managed it.

And now he stood there, looking like a man should look—handsome, confident, charismatic—sending her pulse racing into overdrive. She had no idea how much she'd been wanting to see him until this moment. Correction, how much her *body* had wanted to see him.

"You left your new clothes behind," he drawled, empty-handed.

"I don't need you to buy me clothes," she said coolly as she turned into her apartment, only to find herself twirled back toward him.

Without warning, he kissed her. For heart-stopping seconds she tried to hold something of herself back, but he deepened the kiss. When a faint groan escaped from his throat, she slid into meltdown. Her lips parted.

Just as suddenly he let her go. "Not so cool, eh?" he murmured.

She forced her head to clear. "Talking about yourself?" she challenged.

"Talking about *both* of us."

The nerves in her stomach tightened and she quickly turned into the living room. "How much did you pay the doorman to let you in?"

"He happens to be the father of a friend."

She picked up her purse from the sofa and shot him a look of disbelief. "My, that's quite a coincidence."

He held her gaze. "Yes, it is."

She realized he was serious. Either way, she needed to have some discreet words with the doorman.

"Don't try and get him fired," Jarrod warned.

"Who said anything about getting him fired?" she said in astonishment.

"Oh, I don't know. There's a certain look of revenge in your eyes."

A smirk coated her lips. "That isn't for the doorman."

He gave a husky chuckle, taking her unawares. She wished he'd stop doing that. It was one thing knowing he was enigmatic, quite another to see his more human side. It was best she keep her distance.

She mentally straightened her shoulders. "I'm ready."

His gaze traveled down over her outfit. "I can see why you prefer your own clothes."

She glanced down at her sleeveless, slimline knit dress in vivid marigold, the material lightly rouched at the waist and harmonizing with her hips. It was sexy and flattering and she felt good in it, especially when she combined it with delicate high-heeled sandals in the same color. And heavens, she needed every bit of confidence she could find right now.

She looked back up at Jarrod. "Actually this was a gift from someone."

A cynical look entered his eyes. "A male, no doubt?"

Ah, so they were back to that again. He thought she had conned every man she'd ever met out of something or other.

"Who else?" she retorted, walking toward him. One of the designers had given it to her after a fashion shoot, but she'd let Jarrod think what he liked. It's what he *wanted* to think anyway.

Yet he frowned as she preceded him out of the apartment, and he was still frowning when she closed her door behind them. She hid a small burst of satisfaction. Good. Let him be the unsettled one for a change, even if she had no idea why. It would be too much to ask that he might think he was actually wrong about her.

Her inner poise restored, she headed toward the elevator. "Where are we having lunch?"

"Southbank."

She inclined her head. "Lovely." Lunch at a riverside restaurant would at least surround them with a multitude of people and would take an hour or two out of their day. She dare not think beyond that.

Only, once he'd parked his BMW Coupe in an underground car park in the city center and they rode up the elevator, she realized he was taking her to one of the top hotel restaurants, rather than one of the many places alongside the Yarra River.

Pity it wasn't as crowded as she wanted, she mused as the waiter walked them through luxurious surroundings and seated them at a table for two overlooking the river.

The picturesque city views beyond the glass gave a feeling of spaciousness that would have been delightful if she'd been with anyone else. In Jarrod's company, not even watching the slow-moving riverboats and the strolling couples along the promenade below could put her at ease. The world was still out there but it was hard to notice when she was seated intimately with a man who was now her lover and who intended to remain her lover for three more weeks.

"So," he said, leaning back in his chair once the waiter had departed after taking their order, "tell me about Briana Davenport."

"Read my bio," she quipped, leaning back in her chair, too, pretending to be relaxed.

A corner of his mouth twitched upward. "I want to know about Briana Davenport, the person. Not Briana, the model."

She shrugged her shoulders. "Same thing."

"No, different." He tilted his head, considering her with a slight frown. "I'm just not sure how yet."

"Don't tax yourself thinking about it."

His eyes suddenly narrowed. "So you think I'm only interested in you for your looks?"

She kept her gaze steady. "You mean you aren't?"

A muscle tightened at the edge of his jaw. "No."

Oddly enough, she believed him. But it probably wasn't a good thing to delve too deeply. It would mean having to consider why he was sleeping with her.

"It's a bit late asking me about myself, don't you think?"

He offered her a smile. "I knew enough to sleep with you."

"Hey, don't say that too loud," she whispered, straightening and looking around but seeing there was no danger of anyone's hearing. Thank goodness, she thought, her gaze returning to Jarrod's.

A smile reached his eyes, then was banked. "Okay, let's start again. What do I know about Briana Davenport?" He gave her a silent appraisal. "Hmm. You don't snore."

"I'm pleased."

"You like to snuggle up against a man."

"A natural reaction."

"And you like to be kissed all over."

"Shhh," she hissed.

"It's all true."

"So is the million dollars."

The amusement left his eyes and his gaze hardened, but just as quickly he arched a brow at her. "You don't want to know about me?"

She looked at him long and hard. "I know all there is to know."

"Really?"

She assumed a thoughtful expression. "You have no hesitation in taking what you want."

"True."

"You'll go to any means to get it."

"True."

"You're suspicious of beautiful women."

"True."

"Oh, I forgot. They have to be beautiful *and* greedy."

"Now you're getting there," he said in a dry tone, just as the waiter brought over their first course.

But Jarrod didn't seem fazed by her comment, and after that they ate in silence for a while. She used the time to recover from the constant barrage of awareness Jarrod's presence caused. In her job she was used to being constantly "on," but this was different. Being with Jarrod was being *turned* on.

They had just finished their appetizer when the waiter brought over a bottle of wine.

Jarrod frowned. "I didn't order this."

"No, sir, you didn't. It's compliments of the gentleman over there." The waiter's gaze went across the room to the gray-haired man sitting at a small table by himself, watching them. "For Briana," the waiter added as the older man raised his glass at her.

"Send it back," Jarrod snapped.

"No!" Briana exclaimed, horrified. She speared Jarrod a dark look then smiled at the waiter. "Please pour me a glass," she told him as she got to her feet. "I'll be back in a moment."

"Briana," Jarrod said through gritted teeth.

"Pour him one, too," she instructed the waiter, turning away but not before she saw the glint of humor in the waiter's eyes.

Laughter bubbling within her, her steps were light as she walked across the room with a natural smile on her lips. She couldn't help but feel good that she was winning this battle against Jarrod.

Then she thanked the older man and spent a few minutes talking to him. He turned out to be a fan of hers and was a thorough gentleman.

When she returned to the table, Jarrod's eyes burned through her. "Made an arrangement to meet later?" he snarled.

She shot him a dark glance. This was going too far. "No, but I can go back and ask him, if you like."

"How much did he offer you? One million or two?"

She sucked in a sharp breath. “Don’t be ridiculous.”

“Isn’t that why you went to thank him?”

He sounded jealous, and the thought sent a weird thrill through her. Then she realized this wasn’t about jealousy. This was about belonging to Jarrod Hammond, as temporary as that was.

“He was just being nice,” she said firmly. “He’s a gentleman.”

“He wants to take you to bed.”

“So does most of the male population, I imagine, including yourself.”

A second ticked by, and a smug look crossed his face. “Ah, but *I* did, you see,” he drawled, his voice silky-smooth now.

Her mouth tightened. “I hope you marked it on that belt of yours with all those other notches.”

Sexy amusement flickered in his eyes. “You know something, Briana? I really like fighting with you.”

She ignored that, even as she privately acknowledged enjoying a verbal victory with this man every now and then. “By the way, it’s part of my job as the face of Blackstone’s to maintain good public relations. I wouldn’t want to offend him.”

“As long as they are only *public* relations.”

“If they weren’t, it’s none of your business.”

“Don’t bet on it, sweetheart.”

So, she’d been right to be worried about his thinking he could boss her about. Her chin tilted in defiance. “You don’t own me, despite the million-dollar check.”

His eyes grew cool. “No, but I do own three weeks

of your time. And don't forget you're the one who suggested the million dollars. And you're the one who took the money. I would have just been happy to go to bed with you."

"Yes, and I'm the one who'll pay the price," she said, suddenly feeling sickened by it all. "I think I'd like to leave."

Jarrod's gaze swung across the room. "Won't your number-one fan over there be offended if you don't drink his wine?"

"Oh, you're so right." She picked up the glass and drank it in one go. Thankfully it was only half-full. "There." She put her empty glass back down on the table.

Jarrod's brow rose. "You can handle drinking it that fast, I presume?"

"It was only half a glass." She went to get to her feet but all at once he leaned across the table and put his hand over hers, his touch heating her skin.

"Unless you want our little tiff in tomorrow's papers, you'd better stay here and finish your lunch."

Her forehead creased. "What do you—"

"Here we are, madam," the waiter said, startling her as he slid a plate on the table in front of her. Not that she had much of an appetite by this time. Jarrod seemed to rob her of that once again.

The waiter walked around to Jarrod and did the same. "If there's anything else you would like—"

"No," Jarrod cut across him. "We're fine."

"Very good, sir." The younger man left them alone.

Jarrod waited a moment before speaking. "I saw your

fan talking to some guests at the table over there. They've been checking us out, so I wouldn't be surprised if he said something about the bottle of wine. If you get up and storm out it'll be in tomorrow's paper."

"Maybe you shouldn't have acted like a jealous husband, then," she said without thinking.

He actually looked surprised. "Is that what I sounded like?"

"Either that or a jerk," she said as the rush of wine made her feel a little light-headed.

He grinned. "I think that wine's gone straight to your head."

"No."

"Yes," he insisted.

"Okay, just a little," she acknowledged, finding it easier to give in this time. "But I'm used to it."

"Really?" he mocked.

"I don't have a drinking problem, if that's what you're implying." But somehow she couldn't seem to summon up much anger. She was beginning to feel relaxed and mellow. And, oh my, Jarrod Hammond really was a hunk. And that slow smile…combined with his expert hands…

"I think we'd better finish lunch," he said, breaking into her thoughts, "then I'll take you home."

Would he make love to her?

"Come on, eat. It'll soak up some of that wine. The media would have a field day if they heard the face of Blackstone's was drunk *off* her face."

That brought her out of her trance. He was right. It

could jeopardize her contract renewal. And then she wouldn't have the money to repay Jarrod....

She took a steadying breath, picked up her fork and started eating. Not long after, Jarrod began speaking of general things and she was glad to answer. Polite conversation she was used to. Personal, she was not.

She refused dessert but as they drank their coffee, he sat there looking at her. "How do you feel now?"

"Back to normal. The food helped."

"Good." His eyes took on a sudden sensual warmth that made her heart start hammering. "Now that you're no longer tipsy, I'm going to take you back to my apartment."

Her mouth turned dry. "Why?"

"I want to make love to you. I want you in my bed. Today. Tonight. Right now."

She gave a soft gasp. "Don't say things like that, Jarrod."

"Does it offend you?"

Unfortunately, no.

"It...unsettles me," she admitted, not knowing why she was even admitting that to him.

His gaze took on a piercing look. "I thought you'd be used to men saying they wanted you in their bed."

"Then you'd be wrong."

He gave her a sharp look, as if he had trouble believing that. Then he signaled to the waiter to bring over the check, and before too long they were walking back through the restaurant, through the diminishing crowd of people. The older gentleman had gone, and so had the other people, and that made her wonder if Jarrod had just made that up to keep her here.

But why keep her here when he wanted to take her to his home and make love to her?

And he proved that point as soon as they stepped inside his downtown apartment. She had a glimpse of luxurious surroundings before he swept her up in his arms and carried her into his bedroom.

"I almost hate to take this dress off you," he said in a gravelly voice, slipping it over her head anyway. "It's so very sexy." His gaze slid down over her bra and panties. "*You're* very sexy."

And then he pulled her toward him and his lips found hers, his kiss flooding her with want and need and must haves. Before too long she was aware of a mattress giving way beneath her, of his hands cupping her breasts, touching her secret parts. Then he entered her in one swift movement. When he started to move inside her, hard muscle against soft satin, desire exploded inside her. Finally…finally…he consumed her.

It was dark when she woke and she had to gather her bearings. Her job took her all over the place, so she was used to waking up in strange beds. Alone.

"It's eight-fifteen," a deep male voice rumbled in her ear.

Jarrod!

"At night?" She should move, instead of lying there in the curve of his shoulder, her face pressed against his warm skin.

"I suppose we could be having an eclipse," he joked in a husky voice, his sense of humor surprising her. It wasn't something that came to mind with this man.

She stayed where she was. She couldn't seem to find the energy to move. "Why didn't you wake me?"

"I've been asleep, too. Neither of us got much sleep last night, remember?"

Everything came flooding back. The casino. The million dollars. Being possessed by this man.

Suddenly panicked, she lifted her head. "I'd better get back to my apartment."

"Why?"

She looked up at him in the dim light, trying to focus, trying to think, but it was hard when "God's gift to women" was beneath her. "Um—so I can go to—"

"Bed? You're already in bed. With me."

She moistened her lips. "I need to shower and get something to eat."

"No problem. I'll order in pizza. We'll sit on the balcony and watch the Moomba fireworks light up the sky." All at once, he put her away from him and rolled out of bed. Naked. And then he pulled her up on her feet. Naked.

"What are you doing?"

He bent and scooped her up in his arms. Naked. "We're going to take a shower first."

"Together?"

His brow rose as he carried her into the bathroom. "You have a problem with that?" he said, his blue eyes sure she wouldn't object.

And for once she didn't. "No."

He gave her a look of mild surprise. "Sweet acquiescence?"

She nodded. "Maybe."

His eyes dropped to her mouth. "I think I like it."

Her heartbeat accelerated. "Don't get too used to it."

"That's good. Because I kind of like that snappy Briana Davenport, too, remember." He stood her inside the glass cubicle and picked up the soap. "And now, let's see what type of fireworks we can make for ourselves tonight."

She opened her mouth to jokingly point out that water would put out any fireworks, but his kiss stole her words away. Before too long she didn't care anyway. She went up in flames first, then he joined her, and it proved one thing. They were combustible together, wet or not.

Afterward, he left her on the bed and walked out of the room with a towel wrapped around his hips, saying he'd be back shortly. Satiated but trying not to show it too much, Briana pulled the edge of the comforter over her nakedness. It was silly to even consider hiding her body, but she was still tingling from his touch. She had been putty in his hands. And that wasn't good. Not good at all.

He was back in a few moments, carrying a woman's robe. He came over to the bed and held it open for her, but she stared at the oyster-colored silk as if it carried the bubonic plague.

"Don't worry. It's new."

"Order in a supply, did you?" she said, relieved not to be offered something worn by one of his previous lovers. Then she saw the label still attached to the sleeve.

She glanced up at him. "This is one of the pieces you bought at the casino."

"Yes."

She almost said something about his getting his money's worth, but she didn't want to bring that up. Not right now. Not after he'd made such wonderful love to her. Besides, her brain was tired from fighting.

She let her mouth ease into a smile. "I hope you don't plan on me wearing them all."

A surprised glint of amusement appeared in his eyes. "That was my intention."

"Good luck," she quipped, throwing the cover aside in an attempt to be blasé. Then she got up and slipped into the robe. "You're going to need it, mister."

A moment's silence met her ears, and she looked back at Jarrod behind her, only to find his eyes dark with desire.

He turned her in his arms to face him. "Lady, having you in that robe is all the luck I need," he murmured huskily, his gaze raking down her bare skin exposed by the open gown, making slow warmth heat her cheeks.

"Um…what about the pizza?"

"They deliver late."

He kissed her then and it turned her inside out, and soon he had slipped the robe back off her shoulders, slowly, slowly making love to her once more.

As Briana watched him enter her, she knew one thing. It was wonderful to be wanted by a man who wanted *her.* Not just Briana, the model.

Five

The sound of muffled voices out in the living room woke Briana the next morning, but it was the angry undertone in Jarrod's voice that made her sit up and listen. She hadn't quite heard that disdainful tone before. She'd been the recipient of his derision, but his voice held so much contempt she felt sorry for the other person.

"This is the last time, Anita," he was saying now, in a firm tone that brooked no argument.

"How can you say that, Jarrod? I'm your mother," a woman's voice said tearfully, making Briana gasp.

"You are *not* my mother. My mother is back in New Zealand looking after my sick father."

"And who gave you the opportunity to be a Hammond?" Anita said, her tone coldly unemotional now. "If it hadn't been for me, you would never have been given that silver spoon in your mouth."

He made a harsh sound. "Yes, I suppose that's the only decent thing you ever gave me."

"There you are, then. You should be grateful."

"Anita, don't pretend you gave me up for adoption for *my* sake. It was for *you,* and *you* alone."

Briana was out of bed by this time and slipping into the silk robe, curious in spite of herself. She had to see what Jarrod's real mother looked like.

"That may be so," Anita was saying as Briana tiptoed up to the bedroom doorway. "But I need money, Jarrod, otherwise I'll lose the house."

"That's not my concern," he snapped, as Briana carefully peeked around the doorframe and saw a petite, well-dressed blonde facing her hostile son. But even from here, Briana could see the hardness in her face. It was written clearly in her eyes and in the tight way she held her mouth. This woman was out for all she could get.

"You can spare ten thousand dollars for a loan, Jarrod. You probably make that much money every time you go to sleep."

"I work hard for my money. I invested it well."

"We're not all good money managers, son."

"Don't call me that," he growled, then swore and strode over to his briefcase and took out his checkbook. "This is it, Anita. This is all you're getting." He quickly wrote out the check, then shoved it at her. "Now here. Take it. And don't ever come back."

The woman greedily snatched the check, read the

amount, and her eyes widened with glee. She folded the paper and put it in her handbag. "I won't come back. I promise." A minute later, she left without a word of thanks, or regret, and Briana's heart squeezed with hurt for Jarrod. He didn't deserve a mother like that. No one did.

"You can come out now, Briana."

She stepped away from the door with as much aplomb as she could. "How did you know I was there?" she asked, moving into the living room.

"I heard the swish of your walk."

"Oh, you did not," she chided, slightly embarrassed. He'd been much too busy with Anita.

"I did." His eyes slid over her with lazy sensuality. "Like now."

The arm of the sofa was close by, so she casually sat herself down on it, her knees weak. Then she took a breath and concentrated on the woman who had angered him so much. "She'll come back, you know."

All at once, he turned toward the patio door, but not before she'd seen the bleakness in his eyes. "Yes, I know."

"Will you give her more money?"

His shoulders stiffened but he didn't turn around. "No. She's gotten enough out of me over the years."

She soaked up this information as she considered the tense line of his back beneath the gray polo shirt and black trousers. His clothes may be casual but their quality wasn't. Neither was the tumultuous feelings he must hold inside him.

"How long have you known her?" she asked, not sure he would share any information with her.

He remained where he was. Then, "Anita first came looking for money in my early twenties."

Her heart softened with sympathy. How terrible that his mother had come looking for money, and not her son. "Does she come often?"

"She turns up every couple of years and asks for a 'loan,'" he said, and this time he did spare her a look over his shoulder, his eyes filled with cynicism.

Briana stood up and went beside him. "You don't owe her anything," she said quietly.

"I know."

She put her hand on his arm. "But I guess it's hard to cut ties, no matter what she's done to you."

He glanced at her, put his hand over hers. "She never hesitated to give me up, you know," he said, surprising her with the admission. "She told me so the first time I met her. She said she'd been young and single, and a baby would have tied her down, and she'd had no intention of giving up her freedom."

Briana winced at the other woman's insensitivity. She hated thinking how he must have felt when he discovered she had so easily given him away. Up until then he had probably given his mother an excuse, some leeway, as to why she'd given him up. But to face the reality that she just hadn't wanted a baby, hadn't wanted *him,* and worse, that she hadn't cared, must have been a dreadful shock.

"She's just selfish, Jarrod. Lots of single mothers keep their babies, even back then."

He dropped his hand and turned to face her. "Exactly. If she'd given me up for *me,* then I could have forgiven her. But it was all for her." His jaw clenched. "I was better off without her."

"Absolutely." She paused, not sure whether to ask or not. "What about your real father?"

He shrugged. "Apparently he died years ago."

She arched a brow. "You were never curious about him?"

"No. Should I have been?" He grimaced. "Look, I was never curious about my birth parents. Never. I had a terrific upbringing and so did Matt. As far as I'm concerned, Katherine and Oliver Hammond are my real parents and Matt is my real brother."

Her throat almost closed up for a moment. "Good for you," she said huskily, and meant it. She was beginning to see a new side to the Hammond family that was no longer tarred by Marise's somewhat sarcastic comments. Not that she hadn't liked the Hammonds when she'd met them at Marise's wedding and the few times since. Only, now she could see a different dimension to them, and she liked what she saw.

She gave a slight smile. "It may sound crazy, but when I first heard how Howard believed his kidnapped son was alive, I thought for a moment it might have been you."

Jarrod snorted. "There's a thought. Son to Anita Stirling or Howard Blackstone? What a choice!" He shook his head. "No, I'm afraid I'm not the missing heir to the Blackstone fortune. Thank God!"

Briana had to agree with him. He'd been adopted by the Hammonds, raised by the Hammonds—he was a Hammond. To find out he actually belonged to his family's enemy would have been hard to take. And now that she knew how cruelly his mother had abandoned him, the blow would be doubly hard.

Not that he wouldn't rise above it, she knew, admiration stirring inside her with a new understanding of this man.

He put his hand under her chin, and for one heart-stopping moment held her gaze. Then he leaned forward and kissed her softly on the lips.

"Thank you," he said, lifting his head.

"For?"

"Listening. Understanding."

Her stomach fluttered like a butterfly's wings. "I'm told I have a good ear for listening."

He lifted a finger and ran it around her ear. "They're beautiful ears. Perfect." He placed his lips against it, then gently tugged at her lobe with this teeth.

She groaned as his lips began making their way down her throat. "Um—weren't we going to the—"

Where were they going?

Oh yes.

"—Moomba Festival?" she finished.

"After."

"After?" she murmured.

"After we make love."

Regardless of the way Jarrod made love to her—with a passion that hadn't diminished despite the numerous times he'd taken her in the last thirty-six hours—Briana didn't deceive herself that anything had changed.

And obviously he'd thought the same. He certainly seemed in a hurry to dress and leave the room afterward, saying he had some work to do before they went to the festival. That was probably so, but she suspected he needed some time to himself. It wasn't every day a man like him let a woman see his vulnerable side.

Still, she was relieved he had put up that wall of reserve again. It made her remember that the only reason they were together right now was the money.

So why fool herself that what she knew about him now made any difference? His dislike of the woman he thought she was hadn't changed. He still put her in the same category as Marise—and as his mother.

Having met the older woman, Briana felt doubly insulted. She got out of bed, showered and dressed in one of the outfits Jarrod had bought in the casino. It was either that or put on yesterday's clothes.

Then she left the bedroom and poured herself a much-needed cup of coffee. She was standing with her back against the black granite counter and sipping the hot liquid when Jarrod spoke from the doorway.

"You look great."

She glanced up into his approving gaze. "Thanks," she said somewhat sourly.

"I mean it," he said, obviously sensing her withdrawal.

"I know."

"And?"

"What do you want me to say, Jarrod? That I've been waiting all my life for you to come along and tell me how wonderful I look?"

His forehead creased in a deep scowl. "What's the matter with you?"

She took a deep breath and told herself to take things easy. Okay, so nothing had changed, but then had she really wanted it to? Besides, if he wanted to consider her a money-hungry gold-digger, then nothing she said or did would change his mind.

She pasted on a sickly sweet smile. "How can there be anything wrong when everything is so right?"

He shot her a wry look. "Yes, I can see that," he mocked, but there was also a guarded look in his eyes, as if he suspected she was feeling hurt because he'd shut her out after they'd made love.

Well, she wasn't.

She placed her cup on the sink and tried to sound casual as she said, "I know it's out of our way, but can we go to my apartment first? I'd like to get my camera so I can take some pictures of the festival."

His eyes gave a flicker of surprise. "I have a camera you can use."

"No, that's fine. I'd prefer to use my own camera. It's a very expensive one."

"And you think mine isn't?"

She conceded the point. "A camera's a rather—personal thing."

He scrutinized her response. "I never thought of it that way." Then studied her further. "You like taking pictures, do you?"

All at once she felt uncomfortable. "It's a change from being on the other side of the lens."

He stared hard for a moment longer. "Give me five minutes, then I'll be ready to go," he said, and turned and walked into his study.

An hour later, they'd found a good vantage point along Swanston Street. The Moomba Festival was Australia's biggest community festival and a Melbourne tradition for over fifty years, with firework shows, outdoor movies, the Moomba parade and lots of water-related activities on the Yarra River.

The parade was the highlight of the Moomba Festival and Melbourne families turned out in droves, creating a sea of color and excitement.

The celebrations continued in Alexandra Gardens and along the riverfront, with live entertainment, roving performers and water sports. Briana strolled next to Jarrod, clicking her camera whenever she saw something of interest. She particularly liked taking pictures of people's faces when they were unaware of it. She loved to capture the wondrous expression of a child watching a magician, or the parents watching that child with such love on their faces.

"Don't you get sick of people looking at you?" Jarrod asked after she'd taken a picture of a group of people who'd kicked off their shoes and were having dancing lessons.

She looked at him, startled. "Do they? I hadn't noticed."

"Everyone's recognizing you."

"Maybe it's the camera. Maybe they think I'm someone important."

"You *are* someone important."

She laughed that aside. "Only to my father."

He looked at her a moment or two, a rare, soft light entering his eyes.

Her heart skipped a beat. "What's the matter?"

"You are."

"Why?"

He gave a slight smile. "Maybe one day I'll tell you."

Just then someone jostled them and the moment was broken. She quickly glanced down and pretended to check a setting on the camera, his comment reminding her there never was going to be a "one day" for them.

When she looked up again, she trained her camera on some children having their faces painted. The thought that she and Jarrod were going their separate ways at the end of the month brought an unwelcome lump to her throat. Yet she didn't want to feel even the slightest bit miserable about that. So why did she?

"Do you like being a model?" Jarrod asked as they continued their stroll in the sunshine.

She stumbled a little and he put his hand out to steady her. "That's an odd question." She could feel his warm, firm touch through her sleeve. "Why do you ask?"

"You seem to have quite a talent behind the camera."

She was surprised by his perception. "Thank you. I enjoy it."

"Perhaps it'll turn into more than a hobby."

"Perhaps," she agreed in a noncommittal voice, and moved to take another photograph, making Jarrod drop his hand from her arm. She felt awkward, being unused to sharing her dream with anyone. Not even Patrick had noticed her talent for taking pictures. He'd been too busy complaining she had been ignoring him.

Just then she spied a vendor selling hot dogs, and her stomach growled, reminding her she hadn't eaten. "Hey, how about we get some hot dogs for lunch?"

"Pizza last night, hot dogs today. Sure you don't want to go to a restaurant?"

"No, this is fine." She glanced around. "Let's grab some food and go sit on that bench down there on the riverbank."

"Good idea."

A few minutes later, Briana placed her camera on the bench between her and Jarrod to keep it safe, and then she began eating her hot dog.

"You look like you're enjoying that," Jarrod remarked.

She nodded. "I am."

His eyebrow rose a fraction. "So you don't watch your weight?"

"Of course I do, but sometimes I like to break out." She prided herself on the fact that she wasn't anorexic thin like some of the other models. "Still, in the last two days I've eaten enough junk food to last me six months."

His gaze swept over her. "You've got the perfect figure."

She wondered why she didn't care about any other man's compliment, but Jarrod's stirred awareness inside her.

"Then maybe I should be the body of Blackstone's," she joked. "Perhaps I'll even get them to include that in my next contract."

A curious look came into his eyes. "So they're

offering you another contract, then?" he asked in a measured tone.

"I expect so." Her forehead creased. "You sound surprised. Why?"

There was a short pause. "I thought with all the controversy lately, the Blackstones might—"

"Drop me like a hot potato?" she cut across him, stiffening.

He inclined his head. "Something like that."

She suppressed a shiver, refusing to think right now about *not* being offered a new contract. So far no one had held Marise's antics against her. "You may not have noticed, but I was at Kim Blackstone's wedding. I'd like to think that was a good sign."

"Oh, I noticed," he drawled, a sexy timbre to his voice. "And yes, definitely a good sign."

Still, she needed to reiterate something. "Jarrod, as much as you don't like the Blackstones, they *are* professionals."

The lines of his face turned instantly rigid. "Howard Blackstone was never professional," he rasped.

That may be so but, "He was always good to me," she felt obliged to point out.

"And Marise?" he sneered. "Was he good to her, too?"

She sucked in a sharp breath. "What are you implying?"

"What everyone else is implying, Briana. That they were lovers."

"You have no proof."

His gaze sliced over her. "No, but a woman usually

doesn't leave her husband and child to spend time with another man just to be friends."

"Don't," she whispered, feeling a stab of fresh pain. She looked toward the river and away from Jarrod.

God, she hated to think about her own sister doing something like that, but she suspected he was right. She had tackled Marise about being seen with Howard, but had received a smug comment that she didn't know what she was talking about.

Perhaps if they'd been closer as sisters, Marise would have come to her when she and Matt were having problems. Only, they weren't close, and Briana had always felt guilty about that, yet realistically she knew she couldn't do anything about it. Marise had been her own worst enemy. She'd held people at a distance, then pulled them close when she wanted something from them. She knew her sister's faults as much as anyone.

Of course, it still didn't stop her from thinking that if she had been there for her sister, perhaps Marise might not have been with Howard on that plane…might not have died. It was a sobering thought.

"Was she having an affair with him, Briana?"

She looked back at Jarrod, held his gaze, definitely not appreciating the demand in his tone. "How do I know?"

A hint of anger entered his eyes. "You were her sister."

"Her sister. Not her keeper." A knot lodged firmly in her throat. "Look, Marise was my sister and I loved her dearly. And whatever she did, she did for a reason. I have no doubt about that."

Seconds ticked by. "She doesn't deserve your loyalty. She certainly wasn't loyal to my brother. Or to her son."

Briana bit her lip. She knew he was right but she couldn't say it out loud. She just couldn't betray her sister's memory in this way. She owed Marise a sister's loyalty and understanding. Somehow.

"How *is* Matt?" she asked quietly, trying to remain composed. "And Blake? Is he okay?" She hadn't seen Matt since Howard's funeral so she had no idea how her little nephew was doing. The poor little guy must be missing his mother terribly.

"As well as can be expected." Jarrod sent her a hard look, as if everything that had happened was *her* fault. "Rachel Kincaid is looking after him."

She tried to push his silent accusation aside. "Rachel Kincaid?"

"She's a nanny. Her mother is my parents' housekeeper."

She nodded. "Oh, yes. I remember her name now." She'd never met Rachel, but if Matt thought she was good enough to look after little Blake, then that was good enough for her.

A shutter came down over Jarrod's face. "The only decent thing to come out of all this was Blake."

Everything inside her squeezed tight with anguish. It was all such a mess. If only she could go back and somehow help change things. "I agree."

"Your sister left a legacy of heartache, Briana," he said in disgust, then tossed his half-eaten hot dog into the garbage bin a few feet away.

She winced inwardly, knowing it wasn't the food that disgusted him. "I know she did." Her own appetite totally lost now, she stood up and threw her own partially eaten hot dog in the bin before picking up her camera. She didn't bother to take the lens cap off, having lost her hunger for taking any more pictures today, as well.

After that, they walked around for another hour or so, watching the water-skiers and the bands playing music, but the day was flat now. She was quite relieved when Jarrod suggested he take her home, then oddly disappointed when he walked her to her door but only took a few steps inside her apartment.

"You're not staying?" she said before she could stop herself.

"No."

So that was that.

Weekend over.

She squared her shoulders and met his gaze. "This isn't going to work, Jarrod."

He shot her a level glance. "Yes, it is."

"But—"

"We had a deal, Briana. You'll be my mistress until the end of the month. But you'll be happy to know you're getting a small reprieve. I'm off to Singapore tomorrow for a conference."

"Singapore?" Relief warred with disappointment once more, and she told herself not to be silly. Just because he would be away shouldn't mean a thing. And because the following week she had to go to Brisbane, she should be happier about their having less time together.

So why wasn't she?

"What are your plans for next weekend?" he said, as if she had a choice in the matter.

She frowned. "I'm going to the Grand Prix on Sunday. I'm invited to lunch at the Blackstone corporate box."

He nodded to himself. "Okay, that'll work out well then. My plane lands just after lunch and I'm meeting some business acquaintances at one of the corporate boxes. I want you to join me as soon as you've finished with the Blackstones."

Surprise kicked in. "You don't mind being seen with me at a public function?"

He shrugged. "We'll be in a corporate box together, that's all."

"It could cause speculation in the papers," she warned.

"We'll worry about that when and if it happens."

She tilted her head, not exactly sure why they should bring attention to themselves.

"I'll call you on your mobile phone when I arrive at Albert Park," he said, cutting through her thoughts. "Make sure you take a taxi there because I intend taking you home."

All at once his arrogance got to her. "Is that another way of saying we'll be having sex afterward?" she snapped, deliberately sounding crude and as offensive as him.

His dark look said he didn't appreciate her comment. "I don't need to take you home for sex."

"No, you only need a checkbook."

"Shut up about the bloody money, will you?" he growled.

Her mouth dropped open in surprise, yet she'd seen a glint in his eyes that made her wonder who was more shocked by his reaction.

Then he appeared to bounce right back to his usual arrogant self. He gestured toward the telephone on the side table. "Answer your messages."

With difficulty, she drew her gaze away from his face, seeing the red light flashing on her answering machine. "They can wait."

He arched a brow. "Hiding something?"

She thought of her father and could feel herself blush a little. "No, of course not."

He looked at her sharply. "This deal of ours works both ways, Briana. Don't play me for a fool."

"I don't 'play' people, Jarrod," she told him, chin in the air.

"Is that so?" he said, not looking convinced, reminding her that once again memories of Marise rose between them. And it showed Briana that sex and mutual attraction were really all she and Jarrod had going for them.

She stepped aside but he pulled her into his arms. "No kiss goodbye?" he murmured silkily.

Not giving her a chance to reply, his mouth claimed hers in a hard, brief kiss that seemed to punish rather than enjoy. She pushed at his chest, and the pressure of his mouth eased…and then eased some more…and suddenly they were in the middle of a long, languorous kiss that did delicious things inside her blood, pulsing it through every pore of her skin, leaving his mark.

Eventually he put her away from him. "I look forward to having you in my bed again."

Then he headed for her door and closed it behind him, leaving her standing there for a moment, still tasting him in her mouth. Oh heavens. She looked forward to being back in his bed, too.

Thankfully the winking light on her answering machine drew her attention, and she pulled herself together and hurried to listen to the message. Nothing from her father, but Jake Vance had been in town for a couple of hours today and thought they might have lunch if she called him back before he left for Sydney again.

She discovered that Jake had also left the same message on her mobile phone, and she sighed with a hint of regret. She'd accidentally left her mobile on the sofa when she'd come rushing in earlier to get her camera. It would have been so much easier spending time with any man other than Jarrod. But she was committed to Jarrod now. Totally and irrevocably.

Until the end of the month anyway.

Six

Briana had attended the Grand Prix last year, so had previously witnessed the sensation of the world's fastest men racing at incredibly high speeds around the track. It was a four-day action-packed extravaganza of on-and-off-track activities, culminating in the main race on Sunday.

She knew the layout of the corporate boxes above the pit. Thankfully fumes weren't a problem but ear plugs were supplied for use during the races. Invitations were at a premium, so there was always a good turnout of high-profile guests.

Kim and Ric were in the box to greet her.

"Briana, hello," Kim greeted with a quick hug. "I was so looking forward to seeing you."

Briana was moved that Kim thought her worthy of a

friendly hug. "You, too." She offered Ric her hand. "Hello, Ric."

He took it. "She's talked of nothing else all week," he said with obvious affection for his new wife.

"I'm sure," Briana said with a wry smile. "How was the honeymoon? You went up to Leura, didn't you?"

Kim gave a happy sigh. "The mountains are just beautiful at this time of year. It was such a perfect time for us."

"But far too short," Ric added.

Kim smiled in appreciation. "Yes, far too short." Then her smile slipped a little, and her eyes held a hint of worry. "Unfortunately we couldn't take any longer."

Briana knew Kim must be thinking about the fallout from her father's death, and the many rumors in the business community, including the mysterious buy-up of the company shares.

Ric looped his arm around Kim's waist and pulled her in tight next to him. A look of support passed between husband and wife, confirming they would be okay no matter what happened to Blackstone's. They deserved their happiness.

Just then, Ryan Blackstone and Jessica Cotter came through the door. Pregnant with his twins, Jessica looked happy and healthy, with a still small baby bump.

Briana felt a lump in her throat. She was so pleased it had worked out for both couples. She just wished....

No, if she wished for the same thing for herself, then she'd have to find a man who was her soul mate. It had happened for her parents but she didn't really believe that would happen for her.

When most of the guests had arrived, Jessica patted the chair next to hers. "Come and sit down, Briana." She waited as Briana sat on the chair next to her. "Now," she said, lowering her voice. "Ryan and I are getting married next month, so you'd better be able to make it to the wedding, my friend." She named the date.

Delighted, Briana gave Jessica a quick hug, pleased that she would be back from her overseas assignment by then. "I wouldn't miss it for the world, Jess."

Jessica beamed. "Great. It's all going to be hush-hush, but I'll let you know the details later." She waited while the waiter passed behind her chair, then, "So what's happening with the diamonds? Have you heard back from Quinn yet? You dropped them off at his office after the wedding like you said, didn't you?"

Briana nodded. "Yes, I left them with his office manager. But I haven't heard anything so Quinn must still be away. He said it would be a few weeks." She'd had so much going on that she hadn't given the diamonds any thought. Being Jarrod's lover had kept her fully occupied.

And then some.

Even this past week she'd found herself thinking what he was doing at the conference in Singapore. He hadn't called, but she hadn't really expected him to.

Or had she?

Okay, so she had. She understood being busy, but just a quick phone call to say hello would have been thoughtful. After all, didn't being a temporary mistress afford her some consideration?

Obviously not.

"Is everything okay?" Jessica suddenly cut across her thoughts. "You look a little bit—oh, I don't know—tense."

Tense? That was an understatement. Trust Jessica to see through her.

"You're seeing someone, aren't you?" Jessica said, excitement in her voice.

"Kind of."

Jessica stared at her, then just as quickly pulled a face. "You're not back with Patrick, are you?"

Briana snorted. "Wash your mouth out with soap, Jessica Cotter."

"Thank heavens! That guy was such a sleaze."

Briana felt more than a flicker of surprise. "Why didn't you say something when I was going out with him?"

"Sweetie, you had stars in your eyes. Nothing I said would've mattered."

Briana cringed inwardly. That was probably true.

"So who's making you so tense?"

Briana thought about whether to tell Jessica or not. It was probably going to be in the papers soon enough anyway, once she met with…

"Jarrod," she admitted.

"Hammond?" Jessica squeaked.

"Yes. I'm meeting him this afternoon."

"Here?" At Briana's nod, she sent her a shrewd grin. "That's so great. He's such a hottie. If anyone deserves happiness you do."

"Happiness? Who's talking happiness? I'm meeting the guy for a drink," she fibbed, stretching the truth a little. "It's no big deal."

Jessica wagged a finger at her. "That's what I said when I first went out with Ryan."

Briana opened her mouth to speak, but one of the Blackstone clients interrupted them and she was glad to get off the subject.

She thought it was all forgotten, until Jessica came up to her after lunch and whispered, "He hasn't called yet?"

Briana's mind whirled in surprise. "How did you know he was going to call me?"

"Easy. You keep checking your mobile phone."

"Oh." She hadn't realized she was so obvious.

As if their conversation had conjured him up, Briana's phone rang. Her heart jerked inside her chest as she took the call.

"You answered," Jarrod said in a husky murmur that almost made her forget to take her next breath.

"You expected I wouldn't?" she murmured, keeping her voice low.

"Yes."

"Good." A ripple of anticipation shot through her. "I'm glad I keep you on your toes."

"Actually, I prefer to be lying down. With you."

She caught Jessica looking at her knowingly, and that brought her down to earth in a hurry. "Where are you?" she said, making her tone a shade cooler. If he knew she'd missed him, there'd be no end to his demands.

There was a slight pause. "Just getting out of my car," he said, his own tone cooler now. "Come down the stairs and meet me."

Cooler *and* arrogant, she decided. "Why don't you come up here and get me?"

"Is that wise?"

She realized why. He didn't want to meet up with Kim and Ryan again so soon. They may be cousins but there was still a huge gap between them and him.

"I'm only thinking of you," he added quietly.

He had a point. Why put herself under Blackstone scrutiny and put her contract renewal into jeopardy?

"Maybe this isn't such a good idea," Jarrod said out of the blue, surprising her. He wasn't a man who second-guessed himself, and having him do that now on her behalf made her heartstrings catch.

"Yes, it is," she murmured. "Come and get me, Jarrod."

And suddenly she knew she was doing the right thing. For Jarrod, not herself. For his family's sake he needed to touch base with the Blackstones whenever he could. He'd already attended the jewelry launch and the wedding, so he must at least want to try and breach the huge gulf between the Hammonds and the Blackstones.

She knew that Kim would not hold her involvement with Jarrod against her, short-lived as it would be. She just prayed that Ric and Ryan wouldn't either.

"I'll be there in five minutes," he said, an odd tone to his voice, and ended the call.

Briana turned off her phone and put it inside the pocket of her jacket.

"He's coming here?" Jessica said from behind Briana, startling her again.

Briana spun around. "Yes. I hope no one minds."

Jessica eased into an encouraging smile. "Of course they won't mind. He's family."

Briana ruefully shook her head. "Jess, you know as well as I do that there's family, and then there's *family.*"

Jessica acknowledged the comment with a nod. "Yes, but I think it's time everyone stopped thinking about what Howard wanted and got on with their lives and with what *they* want."

"I think you're right," Briana agreed, as one of the clients came up to talk to her. For the next five minutes Briana chatted with her and Jessica, even as she kept her eye on the door.

And then the waiting was over, and Jarrod walked in the door like he'd never had a moment of doubt. He headed straight for her, making her heart skip a beat. He looked so handsome. So much a lover. And he was hers.

For now.

But before he could reach her, Kim called out his name in a surprised tone. "Jarrod?" She hurried over and kissed him on the cheek. "How lovely to see you here."

"Kim," Jarrod said, acknowledging her, and Briana swore she saw a trace of affection in his eyes for his cousin. She reminded herself that Kim had worked for Matt back in New Zealand, and Jarrod would have gotten to know her over the years. And just because Kim and Matt were now no longer talking…

"What are you doing here? Not that I mind. I just wasn't expecting you," Kim said as Ric and Ryan moved toward the pair, both men frowning.

Jessica went to move, but Briana beat her to it. "He's

come to collect *me,*" she said, stepping forward, just stopping herself from slipping her arm through his. But her chin did angle with a touch of defiance. "Jarrod asked me to accompany him to one of the other corporate boxes and I said yes."

There was a shocked silence.

Kim recovered first with a warm smile. "How nice. But please don't run off just yet. Stay for a drink with us."

Briana watched Jarrod look from Ryan to Ric and back, his shoulders tensing. The two men were standing either side of Kim like a pair of guards. For a moment she thought Jarrod was going to refuse.

"I'd be happy to," he said, his gaze telling the other men he wasn't backing away. That he intended to stay as long as he wanted.

A moment crept by, and it flashed through Briana's mind that perhaps they should leave after all. Jarrod had proven his point.

But before she could say anything, Ric said, "I'll get you a whiskey." He strode away to the bar area and everyone watched him go like he had taken their tongues with him.

Kim asked Jarrod how his parents were doing, and Jessica asked another question, and before too long Ric was back with a whiskey, and talk turned to general things, if a little awkwardly.

Briana stood there and joined in when she could, but she was aware of the speculation in everyone's eyes as they glanced back and forth from her to Jarrod. Did they know she and Jarrod were lovers? Jessica and Kim probably suspected it, but she was certain Ric and Ryan knew. She could see it in their eyes. It was that all-male, all-knowing look that held a new and growing respect for Jarrod for bedding her.

And Jarrod noticed, she was sure. She could tell by the pleased expression on his face. Soon he'd be strutting around like a rooster in a barnyard.

Thankfully Jarrod finished his drink and they took their leave. While Briana was glad to see a slight improvement in the relationship between the men, she didn't like it being at her expense.

As they were heading along the corridor toward the other corporate box, Jarrod drew her into another passageway off on the side where it was quiet.

"What are you—" she began.

He covered her mouth with his for the longest moment, and her legs weakened. She had to grip his forearms to hold herself up.

Eventually he pulled back. "I missed kissing you," he murmured, turning her heart over in response.

She noted he didn't say he missed *her.* He missed *kissing* her. But that's all a man like Jarrod would allow.

"That must be a new feeling for you."

He chuckled in a low throaty sound. "It is actually." Then his gaze lowered over her very feminine, grape-colored suit. "By the way, I love your outfit."

All at once the pleasure on his face reminded her of that rooster look back there. "They know we're lovers, Jarrod."

He frowned. "Who?"

"Ric and Ryan."

His face cleared. "So?"

"You let them think it to boost your ego," she accused.

"No, I didn't."

"You did. You—" He kissed her again, and this time his kiss was even longer and deeper, as if he was trying to stop all thought.

He succeeded.

She sighed deeply with delight.

But when he finally ended the kiss, he didn't wait for her to respond. He took her by the elbow. "Come on. Let's get this afternoon out of the way. I want to take you home and make love to you."

Before she could say anything else, let alone protest, he led her along the corridor until they reached one of the corporate boxes. A Grand Prix staff member immediately opened the door, but not before Briana saw Jarrod's company name on the nameplate. Her head cleared from his kiss.

"You didn't tell me this was *your* box," she said in a low voice as they stepped inside.

He spared her a glance. "Didn't I mention that?"

"No." But then, why should he? If temporary mistresses didn't warrant phone calls from Singapore, then she probably didn't warrant knowing this.

He led her over to a group of men and women about to watch the race. As he began to introduce her, one of the men stood up. "No need to introduce this lovely lady, Jarrod. We all know who Briana is." He smiled at her. "You're certainly a sight for sore eyes, young lady."

Briana put on her model's smile. She didn't always enjoy meeting new people but she never let it show. Most people were genuinely nice.

And then she *did* begin to enjoy herself. And as she saw how the others held Jarrod in high regard, something inside her warmed to him, and before long the incident back at the Blackstone corporate box was mentally filed away. He was a good escort and included her in the conversation, never leaving her side. For a while she let down her guard and forgot all about the family issues between them.

She even caught him watching her with a lazy smile that made her toes curl, and she suddenly felt even more amiable toward him. "I have something to confess. Remember when I said I wasn't taking any of the clothes you bought me at the casino?"

An alert look entered his eyes. "Yes."

"I lied. I took one of the outfits and wore it when I was leaving. I didn't want anyone seeing me wearing the same dress from the night before."

"Obviously you feel safe telling me this while we're in a crowd," he drawled.

"Of course," she said with a shrug and a smile. "But I plan on giving it back to you."

"Keep it."

"No."

"Will you stop being so damn stubborn?" he said in mild exasperation. "The boutique won't take it back, and I certainly have no use for it."

He was right. "Well, when you put it like that…" she

said with a wink, then turned to reply to a question from the gentleman seated on the other side of her.

Jarrod felt the blood rush to his groin at that wink. She'd never been playful before and it had caught him by surprise. He was more than a little charmed, in fact.

Of course he'd always been charmed by her whether she smiled at him or not, he decided as he watched Briana work her magic on his guests during the afternoon. She laughed at exactly the right moments, listened when she needed to, told some modeling anecdotes, and genuinely seemed to be enjoying herself. Not only was she beautiful and intelligent, but he could see that her work ethic was beyond question. She appeared to be a woman with high morals. She wasn't flirting with the other men, or making the women feel less in her presence. Yet he couldn't deny she had slept with him for money.

So why did she appear to have a conscience about that, considering the type of person she supposedly was, according to her sister? That made him wonder now if Marise had been playing games. The other woman had been excellent at stirring up trouble over the years. Certainly she'd played games with Matt, so why not with *him?* More importantly, why had he believed her?

Looking back, all those suggestions about Briana liking money had made sense at the time, but he'd seen no hint of Briana overspending, or of her having a good time now. The Briana he'd been with these past few weeks just wasn't the same person he'd expected from Marise's comments.

Hell, Marise wouldn't have put her Blackstone contract in jeopardy for him as Briana had today. And he sure as hell wouldn't have discussed his adoption with someone like Marise, nor would he have missed Marise like he'd missed Briana in Singapore this past week. It was the reason he hadn't called. He hadn't liked the effect Briana was having on him and he had been determined to ignore it—and her. Now he wished he hadn't. He'd been the poorer for not hearing her sexy voice.

Late afternoon, Jarrod decided to hand over the event to his second-in-charge. They said their goodbyes and were just reaching his BMW when he heard another man call Briana's name. Thinking it was one of her fans he was surprised when a tall, well-dressed man walked up to them and kissed Briana on the cheek.

"Patrick!" she said, and Jarrod saw her face reflect dismay before she quickly schooled her features.

"You're looking gorgeous as ever," this Patrick said, his gaze sliding over her in a way that ate her up.

She glanced at Jarrod as if she knew he wouldn't be pleased, then back at the other man. "What are you doing here?"

"Drinking lots of champagne and enjoying the sights," Patrick said. "And you're one of them." He pulled her toward him and kissed her again. "It's good to see you."

Jarrod watched her step back as fast as she could, and decided it was time to stake his claim. He moved in closer and put his arm around her waist. “Aren’t you going to introduce us, Briana?”

Her mouth tightened, though whether because of him or this Patrick he wasn’t sure. “Jarrod, this is Patrick. He *used* to be my business manager,” she said pointedly.

Definitely meant for Patrick, Jarrod mused. But he could feel her tenseness against him, so it must not have been a friendly parting, on Briana’s part at least.

Patrick’s slyly amused gaze noted his hand on her hip. “Oh, but we were much more than that, weren’t we, Bree?”

Something fierce slammed into Jarrod’s gut when he heard this guy call her the nickname. It confirmed what he’d already suspected.

“Were we?” she said coolly.

Patrick quietly chuckled as he looked at Jarrod. “Women! They never forget a thing.”

Jarrod’s hand must have tightened on her hip because she winced. He relaxed his hold but that didn’t stop the feeling that this other guy was a jerk. For the first time in years he wanted to hit another man.

Patrick didn’t seem to notice anything out of the ordinary. “I’m really sorry to hear about your mother. And Marise, too.”

She inclined her head but her eyes remained cold. “Thank you.”

“Look, I don’t suppose you want to meet up later for a drink,” he said to Briana, and Jarrod had no doubt *he* wasn’t included in the invitation.

“No thanks, Patrick. I’m busy.”

Patrick looked disappointed but there was a cold gleam in his eyes. "Well, if you change your mind, you know how to find me."

Jarrod's jaw clenched. These two had a past and he didn't like it. Not one bit. Nor did he like the implication that Briana could easily call this idiot and slip into bed with him.

"Goodbye, Patrick," Briana said, then walked to the car a few feet away.

Jarrod shot the other man a hard look then followed her. He didn't say anything as he unlocked the car door, then held it open for Briana. By the time he came around the other side, Patrick was no longer in sight.

He wanted to say something to her about it but noted she had a withdrawn look that said she didn't want to talk. He allowed her that. He could wait.

Once inside his apartment, he could wait no longer. "How long were you and Patrick together? As lovers, that is."

Wariness clouded her blue eyes, but her chin lifted. "A year."

"He's the one, isn't he?" he said, sounding calmer than he felt. "He's the one who stole your trust."

"He stole more than my trust," she said with a touch of bitterness, then seemed to freeze.

"Go on."

She hesitated only briefly. "He invested all my hard-earned savings and lost the lot."

Jarrod swore. "How?" Then he listened as she explained what the other man had done. He swore again.

"The guy looks like a con-artist to me. I could check it out for you. I *am* a property lawyer, after all."

"No!" she blurted, then seemed to pull herself together. "Look, I thoroughly checked the paperwork before I handed over anything to him and it was all aboveboard. I realize now he just gets involved in schemes that sometimes work out, sometimes don't. My one didn't."

He suddenly didn't like the way she was defending the other man so readily. "You still have feelings for him?"

A derisive sound emerged from her throat. "To tell you the truth, I don't know what I ever saw in Patrick."

Relief washed through him, but, "Then why defend him?"

"I wasn't. I—" She stopped, and started again. "Look, what Patrick and I had is dead and gone." Her mouth tightened. "And that's all I'm going to say on the matter."

Something wasn't quite right, but he felt that "something" was to do more with Briana than Patrick. He was sure of it. And it occurred to him that perhaps this was the reason she had slept with him.

"So you recouped your losses by taking my million dollars?"

Her eyelids flickered. "Yes. It was the only way I could get some money."

He saw she had hesitated. And that meant she wasn't telling him the truth. At least, not the *whole* truth.

"Why did you take the million dollars, Briana?" he asked silkily.

Her gaze darted past his shoulder, then back again. "You already have your answer, Jarrod."

"Do I?" He recognized evasion when he saw it. He was a lawyer for God's sake. He knew how to respond to a question without actually giving an answer. And she was doing it well.

Too well.

He started to demand she tell him everything, only he looked at the stubborn angle of her chin and knew she had gone as far as she would go right now. He would bide his time.

Yet suddenly time was the one thing that was running out for them. He pulled her close and started to make love to her, a tenseness in him that for the moment had less to do with knowing Patrick had been her lover, and more to do with letting Briana go.

Briana spent the weekend with Jarrod then had a couple of days at her apartment to prepare for her Brisbane trip on the Wednesday. After all, staying in top shape and looking good kept a model busy.

Still, she couldn't shake the unsettled feeling she'd had since seeing Patrick at the Grand Prix. She had hated running into him. He brought back too many unpleasant memories.

But it had been Jarrod's reaction to Patrick that worried her more than the meeting itself. Could he have been jealous? The thought made her feel light-headed, as if the oxygen had just been sucked from the room.

On the other hand, perhaps he just didn't like another

man wanting what he had, especially if it was an ex-lover. Yes, that sounded more like it, she mused, as she stepped out of the shower and heard the phone ringing.

"I'm taking you to the airport," Jarrod said before she could speak.

She frowned. She didn't have to leave for two hours. "But you'll be at work."

"I'm taking you."

"Why? Don't you think I can find it myself?" she quipped, but she felt uneasy. This wasn't just about him being his usual, arrogant self. This was about him having what Patrick wanted.

"Did it occur to you that I just might like to spend a bit more time with you?"

"Actually, no."

There was a small pause. "Your loss," he said and hung up the phone.

Briana winced. Had she misread him after all? She wasn't sure, but she knew he was right about it being her loss. Any woman would think her mad for missing the opportunity to spend more time with Jarrod Hammond.

But she didn't call him back.

And she didn't call him while she was away either. Nor did he attempt to call her.

The three days went quickly, and Briana was more than a little anxious to see how things were between them once she was back in Melbourne.

Her mind was fully on Jarrod when early evening on Good Friday she stepped off the plane at Tullamarine Airport in Melbourne and got the shock of her life.

Patrick was waiting for her as she wheeled her small suitcase through the lounge gate.

Her mouth dropped open. "Patrick! What are *you* doing here?"

He kissed her cheek, a cold smile lifting the corners of his mouth. "Striking while the iron's hot."

Apprehension rushed through her. "What do you mean?"

"We need to talk."

Her misgivings increased. "Now?"

"It would be in your best interests if you did."

A feeling of uneasiness went through her. "Patrick, whatever my interests are they don't concern you any longer." She went to step past him. "Now, if you'll excuse me."

He put his hand on her arm. "Your father may not agree," he warned, his "Mr. Charming" persona wearing thin.

"Wh—what?" He couldn't possibly know. He couldn't. Just couldn't.

"That got your attention, didn't it?" he said, looking pleased with himself. "Come on. Let's talk over a drink."

"But—" She was still reeling. Still trying to take all this in.

"This way," he said, guiding her forward, his hand on her elbow.

Briana was stunned, her mind going over all the possibilities. If he had said anything else, she would have told him to get lost. But mentioning her father was disturbing.

He took her to a bar along the walkway, then sat her

down near one of the large windows where she could watch the planes take off. She wished she was on one of them right now. She had a feeling she wasn't going to like what he had to say.

"How was your flight?" he asked, once he'd bought their drinks.

She glowered at him. "Cut to the chase, Patrick. What do you want?"

A moment passed, his stare drilling into her. "You're going to Asia soon."

Her forehead creased in a frown. "Yes. So?"

"I want to be reinstated as your business manager. I'm coming with you."

She made a derisive noise. "No chance."

"Is that so?" he said, a lethal calmness in his eyes that worried her.

She shook her head, trying to make him see reason. "I don't understand, Patrick. *Why* do you want to be my business manager again? It didn't work out the first time."

He paused, as if deciding how much to say. "Things haven't been the same since we parted. I need to renew some high prestige connections, and two weeks with you in Hong Kong, Taiwan and China should do it."

"Maybe you should have thought of that before you lost all my money in a bad investment," she choked, not in the least sorry for him. Yet she blamed herself, too. She shouldn't have taken his advice and gotten a second opinion.

"It was a good investment, Briana. It just went wrong." Just as quickly, he pasted on a sly smile. "But then, it's easy to get tangled up in something bigger than ourselves at times, don't you think?"

What was he implying? "Look, I don't know what you're hinting at, but just say what you have to say so I can go home."

"Okay then." He waited for effect. "I *know* what your father's been doing."

She tried not to flinch. "And that is?"

"Stealing money from Howard Blackstone."

Her heart dropped to her feet, but she forced herself not to react. Whatever he knew, he may not be certain. "I don't know what you're talking about."

"Don't play games," he said cynically. "Remember last year when your parents went on that world cruise? Remember how you suggested I stay at their house for a week when my apartment flooded?"

"Yes." Surprising how even then she hadn't wanted Patrick moving in with her, not even for a week. She had the feeling she wouldn't get rid of him, and her parents' house had been a blessing. Or so she'd thought at the time.

"I was using your father's laptop one night because mine was having problems—I think some water had got into it," Patrick said in an aside that made her want to snap at him to get on with it. "And I found something interesting. There was some bank information on it that at the time I didn't realize meant much. It's only now that I've put two and two together."

"Really? That's amazing. But I don't know how you can come to the conclusion my father stole from Howard Blackstone."

"Give me a moment to explain," he said as if he was talking to a two-year-old. Then he deliberately took time to sip his drink before answering. "Okay. It was only after I saw you the other day at the Grand Prix I was thinking about that world cruise and how your parents could pay for it. Your father had retired from his job and your mother was dying at the time, only none of us knew it."

There wasn't even a hint of sympathy in his voice, Briana noticed.

"You had no money to spare, either," he continued. "It was all tied up in your investment. And Marise was over in New Zealand, your parents rarely saw her, and I'm sure if she had loaned them the money I would have heard about it."

His touch of cynicism for Marise was justified, Briana admitted. "So?"

"Well, then I got to wondering how your father paid for everything—the cruise, the medical treatments. And it all fell into place. Your father used to be Howard Blackstone's accountant. All those figures and dates and an account called 'Black Rock' got me doing some investigating. And what I discovered was *very* interesting."

Her hand tightened around her wineglass. "You're making this up."

"Fine. Then let's go the police and I'll get them to check things out. I'm sure they'd be more than interested in anything to do with Howard Blackstone and his death in that plane crash."

Her heart slammed against her ribs. "My father had nothing to do with the plane crash!"

"No, but I'm sure they'd have to investigate everything I tell them anyway."

He was right. Even the suggestion of her father being involved in the crash would be enough to have the police checking out everything to do with their lives.

Defeated, she slumped back against the chair. "So you want two weeks as my business manager?"

His eyes flared with triumph. "In writing." He took a piece of paper out of his jacket pocket and slid it across the table like a snake. "Sign this."

She opened the paper and began reading with a numbness that was comforting. "You've certainly thought of everything."

"Everything except you becoming my lover again," he said in a deceptively relaxed voice. "I don't think we need write that down, do we?"

She shoved the paper at him. "No way. That's not part of the deal. I won't sleep with you, Patrick." Why, just the thought of it turned her stomach. After Jarrod....

He fixed her with a stare. Then, "Okay, we won't become lovers," he relented, and pushed the paper back for her to sign. "But I don't want anyone else knowing that. To the world, we're lovers again. It's the only way I'm going to renew my contacts."

Relief washed through her. There was no way she could have given in to that demand. She had slept with

Jarrod because she'd wanted to. That wouldn't be the case with Patrick.

"What happens after the two weeks and they realize we're no longer an item?" she asked.

"By then I'll have signed up Lily Raimond. She's going to be the next big superstar." His lips twisted. "Move over, Briana."

"Gladly."

He considered her. "You never did realize what power you had at your fingertips."

She ignored that as she picked up the pen and signed. "You stick to your end of the bargain and so will I. Otherwise, my father or not, I'll tell the police about your blackmail—and the rape." She watched his face blanch and felt a measure of power. "Because that's what it will be if you touch me, Patrick."

He folded the paper and put it in his jacket pocket. "I don't remember you being so reluctant to be in my arms before," he scoffed but she could see fear in his eyes.

She stood up. "Think again."

Seven

Briana wasn't sure how long she sat in her car at the airport car park. One minute the sun was setting, the next it was dark and the overhead lights were on. She needed some time to think and sort things out. There was no getting around Patrick over this, of that she was certain.

How on earth had he figured it all out? It wasn't like the account had been one of Howard's regular ones. It was a "secret" account, for heaven's sake. An obscure account in the bowels of some banking institution somewhere in the world, which no one had known about except her father, Howard's previous accountant and Howard himself. And the last two men were now dead.

But Patrick was experienced at walking that fine line between legal and illegal, and like a dog who'd sniffed out a buried bone, he had unearthed the one crime committed from her father's lapse in judgment.

Now she had to phone her agent, who would declare her absolutely crazy to even *think* about reinstating Patrick as business manager, let alone doing it.

And then there was Jarrod.

Oh God.

Yet what business was it of Jarrod's anyway, she asked herself a touch defiantly. He only wanted her for the rest of the month, and after that she was free to do what she liked. Even if she wasn't going to be Patrick's lover, it shouldn't matter to Jarrod what she did with the rest of her life.

So why was she worried? She'd end her relationship with Jarrod, go away on assignment with Patrick, and after that it would be rare that she ran into Jarrod again.

And if at some time he heard she was back with her ex-business manager, well, Jarrod hadn't wanted her anyway.

She felt sick at heart at the thought of it all, but despite everything she suddenly wanted to see Jarrod. Wanted to be in his arms, feel his reassuring presence, even if that reassurance was all in her mind.

But as soon as she pressed his buzzer, she knew she'd made a mistake in coming here. The last time they'd spoken, he'd hung up on her for not letting him take her to the airport. And heavens, what if he had decided to come and get her today? If he'd seen her with Patrick and somehow found out about her going away with Patrick, then that meant the end for them now instead of ten days time. Suddenly those ten days were so extra precious…

She turned back toward the elevator just as he opened his door. "Hey, you're not going anywhere," he said, pulling her into his apartment and into his arms. He kicked the door shut behind them and kissed her, and once again she melted into him.

Then he slowly broke off the kiss. "I think I missed you."

Her heart thudded at his words. He wasn't saying he missed *kissing* her, like he'd said last time. This time he missed *her.* Oh Lord. What did that mean? Did he actually have feelings for her?

She prayed not. Jarrod was not for her. Especially now, not with Patrick blackmailing her. Things would be just too complicated.

She swallowed her anxiety and managed to tease him with, "You only think?"

"If I said I missed you for sure, you'd do that female thing and assume you have a hold over me."

He had it wrong. It would be the other way around. "Actually, I wouldn't."

His intense blue eyes riveted on her face. "You really wouldn't, would you?"

"No."

He didn't give her a chance to reply. He began kissing her again and she kissed him back, and suddenly she felt desperate for him. She so badly needed his touch right now. When all this ended she wanted to remember being in his arms.

Afterward, Jarrod came back from the bathroom and sat on the edge of the bed. "You okay?"

She looked away, then back. She couldn't let him find out about Patrick. "I'm fine. Just a bit tired, I guess."

His eyes seemed to probe her own. "Your job's pretty time-consuming, isn't it? Not to mention sheer hard work."

She almost felt dizzy at his words. It wasn't just his acknowledgement of the many hours she put into her job. It was the growing respect in his eyes. She hadn't felt that from him before.

"Yes, Jarrod, it is," she said, knowing that if she had achieved one thing in their time together, it was this.

His gaze held hers for a moment, then, as if he had better things to do, his face went blank and he pushed himself off the bed. "I'll make us something to eat," he muttered.

Briana watched him leave the room and sighed. He may have new respect for her now, but that respect obviously didn't extend to asking if she actually *wanted* to eat.

And right now she wasn't sure she could.

Briana felt refreshed when she woke the next morning, lying spoon-fashion in front of Jarrod, his hand resting on her thigh. She glanced at the clock and saw it was almost ten and suddenly felt guilty for lying in so late. She had things to do today, including visiting her father and preparing for a fashion show next week and—

It all came rushing back with a vengeance then.

She was being blackmailed.

God, how was she going to find the strength of will to get through this? She wasn't sure she even could. No matter how much she tried, her modeling career, her future monies, would always be tied to Patrick now. He would make sure of that.

Next to her, Jarrod rolled onto his back and for a moment she froze. Last night when she'd arrived, he'd kissed her and they'd ended up making love, but she didn't want that to happen this morning. She needed to get moving.

Thankfully, he continued sleeping, and she slid out of bed and pulled on the oyster-silk robe. He'd brought up her suitcase from her car late last night, so she'd shower in the other bathroom so as not to wake him, then dress and leave him to sleep in peace.

Right before she left, she peeked in on Jarrod again. He was still sleeping, the sheet low on his taut hips, his naked chest muscular and arrowed with hair, a dark shadow of hair on his jaw making him look manly, short rumpled hair on his head very sexy. God, he was incredibly handsome.

Then she saw the dark circles under his eyes, and she felt bad for sneaking out like this. As much as she wanted to run, the least she could do was make him breakfast before she left.

Five minutes later, she'd just finished dishing a fluffy omelet onto a plate when she heard a noise behind her. She spun around.

"So…" Jarrod snarled, behind her in the doorway, making her jump, "it's over between you and Patrick, is it?"

One look at his face and at the newspaper in his hand which he must have collected from outside his door and her heart began to thud. Had they found out about her father? Had Patrick told anyway?

He strode toward her and held the newspaper up in her face. "You call *this* being over?"

She placed the frying pan back on the stove and snatched the paper from Jarrod. Then she glanced at the page and groaned inwardly even as relief surged through her. The papers hadn't found out about her father's embezzlement. This was a picture of her and Patrick at the airport bar yesterday. The caption read "Is Briana Doing *Business* With Her Ex Again?"

"Jarrod, this isn't what you think. I—"

"Am playing me for a fool," he said through gritted teeth.

"No!"

"You can't deny it, Briana. You were even wearing the same outfit." He stabbed her picture with his finger to prove his point.

"Jarrod, look, I'm not trying to deny it," she said, struggling to maintain an even tone. "Patrick *was* there at the airport, but he only came to meet me because—"

"He met you!"

"Yes, he was there when I came off the plane. He wanted to discuss something."

"I can imagine," he said, his voice dripping sarcasm.

She ignored that. She had to stay cool, but she had to think quickly. "It's about an assignment at the end of the month. We're both connected to it and needed to discuss it, and I had to sign some paperwork." It was her turn to stab at the picture. "See, I've even got his pen in my hand. And see, that's the paperwork on the table in front of me."

His mouth clamped in a thin line. "Why didn't you mention this last night?"

She handed the paper back to him and squared her shoulders. "I've done nothing wrong. And despite what you think, I don't have to report to you."

"And that's all it was?"

She met his gaze. "Yes," she lied.

"And there's nothing you want to tell me?"

There was plenty, but her hands were tied. "No," she said, concealing her inner turmoil. "Look, do you think if I was having an affair, I would be sitting in a bar in public with my ex-business manager?"

"Perhaps it's what you did after that—" he suggested, evidently not totally convinced of her innocence.

"I came straight here after that. You can check the time my flight landed." She paused. "So you see, Jarrod, *you're* my alibi."

He scowled at her but didn't say anything.

She arched a brow. "So what's the verdict?"

"I'm reserving judgment for the time being."

All at once this was about more than convincing him nothing was going on between her and Patrick. This was about Jarrod believing she wasn't like Marise. About him trusting her, even as a transient in his life. It may not matter to him, but it mattered to her.

"That's not good enough, Jarrod," she said, standing her ground. "You either think I'm guilty or not guilty."

He held her gaze for the longest moment, then expelled a slow breath. "Okay, not guilty."

Something inside her leaped with joy. If he hadn't believed her they could have gone no further in their relationship. She would be out that door without a backward glance, million dollars still owing or not.

He tilted his head. "I just don't understand how you can have dealings with someone who did the wrong thing by you."

"And like you don't deal with people in your world that you dislike?" she gently scoffed.

He stood there for a moment, then nodded. "You're right. My world is full of people I dislike. It comes with being a lawyer." A glint of wry humor entered his eyes. "I'm usually only involved when someone is getting screwed around."

"There you are then. Having dealings with Patrick is just business, Jarrod. He may have lost my money, but he didn't steal it."

He held her gaze a moment more, then, "Fine."

It was time for a diversion. She looked down at the omelet on the plate. "Your breakfast is cold now."

"So I see. Where's yours?"

She shrugged. "I'm not hungry. I was just cooking this for you before going to see my dad."

His eyes went over her tight jeans, thin knit top hugging her breasts, up to her ponytail but he didn't say anything, though she saw an appreciative light come in them. "You go then. I'll heat this up. Thanks."

"You're welcome." She noted he wasn't stopping her,

and that was just as well. Despite them sorting it out she could still feel things were a bit uneasy between them.

"Are you doing anything tomorrow?" he suddenly said.

"No." That meant she must not be seeing him tonight. It was crazy to feel disappointed but it was probably for the best. It was Saturday night anyway, and she'd had a vague plan to invite her father over for dinner.

"Let's go for a drive down the coast and spend the day at the beach. We can enjoy the last of the warm weather."

She blinked in surprise. "As long as you don't expect me to go swimming," she teased, trying not to show how upset she really felt about everything. "The water's far too cold now."

"No, we'll have a picnic." He gave a bit of a smile that seemed forced to Briana. "I'll be disappointed not to see you in a swimming costume."

She could feel her cheeks grow hot and said the first stupid thing that came to mind. "But you've seen me without my clothes."

Oh heavens!

Desire flared in his eyes and nothing seemed forced now. "That I have." He lifted her chin and placed a soft kiss on her lips. "You are so damn beautiful," he murmured, like he'd never get enough of staring at her. "You really don't know how beautiful, do you?"

She gave a self-conscious shrug. "I look in the mirror every day."

He shook his head. "It's hard to believe a woman so beautiful is so totally unaware of herself."

"Well, you know what they say about beauty."

"Skin deep? No, I'm talking about *you,* Briana. Not the model."

Happiness bubbled up inside her, but she kept it hidden. Everything was going to be okay between them. "Well, right now Briana 'the daughter' had better go and see Ray 'the father' so that I can invite him to dinner tonight."

A humorous gleam came into his eyes. "I'll pick you up at noon tomorrow."

Happy, she stepped around him and hurried out of the apartment. That bubbly feeling stayed with her until she walked into the kitchen of her old home and her father told her he was having trouble putting the money back in Howard's account.

Then the bubble burst.

Her heart sank.

"What do you mean, Dad? How can you take the money out but not put it back?"

He tried to look unconcerned, but she knew he was worried. "Some of the accounts are under scrutiny since Howard's death. And I'm just being extra careful." He hugged her. "Now don't you worry, honey. I'll put the money back and then I'm going to get a job to help you pay Jarrod back his loan. It's time I returned to work anyway."

She frowned at him. "Dad, it's okay. I'll be signing my new contract with Blackstone's soon," she said with more confidence than she felt.

"But that's *your* money. You shouldn't have to use it to help me."

"It isn't just for you, Dad. It's for Mum, too."

His eyes softened with tenderness and love. "You're a good girl, Briana." Then pain crossed his face. "I just don't know where we went wrong with Marise. I know your mother felt she needed more attention than you did, but I didn't always agree. We had many a fight over it, you know."

She gaped in shock. "You did?"

He nodded. "I think your mother's attitude helped make Marise the way she was." He gave a shaky sigh. "God help me, but I shouldn't be speaking of the dead this way."

She put her hand on his shoulder and squeezed comfortingly. "Dad, it's okay. I know Mum loved me."

"Yes, she did, honey. Very much," he said in a choked voice, then shuddered and took a deep breath.

Briana waited for him to regain his composure. "You know," she said gently, "we have to put all this behind us now. We can't change the past and we can't beat ourselves up about it." Easier said than done, she knew.

He offered her a hint of a smile. "You're right, honey."

"Of course I am." She pasted on a bright smile. "Now, how about you come around my apartment this evening for a nice dinner? Just you and me."

"That would be great." He paused. "But I don't want to be a bother. I know you have lots of friends and—"

Suddenly she saw the question in his eyes. "Dad, I know you must have seen the newspaper photo of Patrick and me. And no, we're not back together. I was only meeting him because he has something to do with an assignment I'm on at the end of the month."

The worry in his eyes cleared. "Good. I was never real fond of him." He hesitated. "I like Jarrod, though."

They'd never spoken of Jarrod, but there'd probably been a picture or two of her with him at the Grand Prix. She'd seen a couple of journalists clicking their cameras in their direction, and that had made her even more thankful she'd let the Blackstones know she was seeing him. At least there were no surprises.

"I've been going out with Jake Vance, too," she pointed out wryly.

"I know," he said, just as wryly, his comment reminding her she was news no matter whom she dated. "But there's just something about you and Jarrod Hammond."

Yes, and it was called sexual attraction.

"I guess we've bonded over Marise and Matt. Now, what time are you coming over tonight?"

His smile said he realized she was changing the subject. "I'll be there at six."

Jarrod had stood on the balcony and watched Briana's car drive away. Hell, the last few days while she'd been in Brisbane, he'd checked out this Patrick and found the investment made with Briana's money had all been legal, unfortunately. In the end, Jarrod had put it all to the back of his mind.

And then he'd opened the newspaper to the picture of her and Patrick together. He'd felt like someone had punched him in the gut. She'd made a deal with *him* and he expected her to honor that, not go off and jump in the sack with an ex-lover. Even now the thought of it made him see red. She was *his* for the moment.

So he'd had a few bad moments about believing her when she said nothing physical was going on between her and Patrick. But dammit, he was still confused as to why she would do business with her ex-business manager. Did she want to or didn't she have a choice?

His jaw clenched. No, he wasn't going to doubt her. He'd said he believed her and he did. And to be fair, she was right about one thing. There were plenty of people in his world he disliked, but he still did business with them regardless. Why would the modeling world be any different, he asked himself as he went to take a shower, passing by the rumpled sheets on the bed that suddenly made him want her back here.

So why had he let her leave?

Why not spend the rest of the day with her?

And the night as well?

He grimaced. Because the shock of that picture in the paper had made him feel exposed in more ways than one. It had made him admit to himself that for most of the week while she'd been in Brisbane, he'd been unable to concentrate fully on his job. And he hadn't liked it. He'd needed to clear his head, away from the influence of Briana Davenport. She'd had far too much influence over his feelings lately. More than any other woman he'd ever known. And that was detrimental to a fleeting relationship.

Just after lunch the telephone rang. It was Danielle Hammond, bringing thoughts of family to the forefront of his mind, which was just as well. He'd been trying to concentrate on a client's case, but Briana kept coming to mind.

"I thought I'd give you a call, Jarrod," Danielle said warmly but quickly, as if she half-expected him to hang up on her. "Mum and I are here in Melbourne for some Easter shopping and I thought it might be a good opportunity to have dinner together at the casino tomorrow night."

Jarrod's brows drew into a frown. He'd planned on spending the evening with Briana after taking her to the beach, and he didn't really want to share her with anyone. Still, Danielle was his cousin, and he liked her and Sonya more every time he met them.

"Mum said she'd been disappointed that she hadn't really spoken to you much at Kim's wedding, or at the jewelry launch," Danielle continued. "She really wants to get to know you."

"Does she?"

"We're family, Jarrod," she pointed out, and Jarrod realized she had taken his comment the wrong way.

Dammit, Howard Blackstone had a lot of things to answer for in breaking up the families like this all those years ago. None of it should ever have gotten to the stage where family had been set against family. Hammond against Hammond.

"Dinner will be fine."

"Great!" Danielle said. "And hey, can we keep it a secret from my mum? I'd like to surprise her. She'll be so happy."

Jarrod had to smile at her enthusiasm. "If that's what you want."

"It is. Oh, and Jarrod—" She hesitated, then, "If you'd like to bring Briana, we don't mind."

His smile disappeared. Obviously they'd been reading the newspapers and knew Briana had accompanied him to the Grand Prix. No doubt Kim or Jessica Cotter would have mentioned it, too.

"Of course," Danielle continued, "if she's with someone else—"

"She isn't," he said firmly, knowing she meant Patrick. "Briana will be with me."

"Wonderful. We'll see you tomorrow night."

Jarrod said goodbye, but as he ended the call he realized Danielle may not have meant Patrick at all. She could have meant Jake Vance.

Either way, both men were going to miss out.

Briana enjoyed having dinner with her father that night, but by the time Sunday morning rolled around she couldn't help but wonder how things stood between her and Jarrod now. After their confrontation yesterday, would Jarrod have second thoughts about believing her over Patrick?

But when she opened the door to him at noon, her fears were laid to rest. He presented her with a huge Easter egg.

"Ooh, I love chocolate," she gushed, feeling a giddy sense of pleasure, not just for the gift, but because it seemed like a peace offering. That meant things could get back to normal for them for their remaining time together.

"Some women prefer diamonds," he said, watching her.

Her excitement faded. Yes, they were back to normal all right. She angled her chin. "Not me."

His gaze became guarded. "I'm beginning to realize that," he muttered, then just as fast said, "Are you ready to go?"

For a split second she thought she'd misheard his first comment, but then realized she hadn't. He really was beginning to believe that she wasn't a money-hungry female on the prowl for a good time.

Silly tears of relief pricked at her eyes. "I'll just get my things," she said, spinning away and pretending to check through her beach bag. Did this mean he didn't think she was like Marise any longer? Was it bad of her to be grateful if that were the case? "I wasn't sure what to bring," she nattered on.

"Just yourself."

She blinked to get control of herself, picked up her sun hat and bag, then looked up with a smile. "Ready."

His gaze slid over her body in Bermuda shorts and a tank top. "*More* than ready," he said huskily, making her shiver with awareness.

She went to take a step toward him then stopped, her eyes drawn to what *he* was wearing. Her stomach did a flip.

"What are you looking at?" he asked, something lazily seductive in his voice.

"You. I can't believe you're wearing jeans." She'd never seen him dressed quite so relaxed before.

He broke into a smile. "I'm just a man."

She returned his smile. "Yeah sure."

After that, an inane sense of joy wrapped around her heart. She knew it couldn't last—happiness never did—but today she was determined to hold onto the feeling as long as she could.

The drive down the Surf Coast was pleasant in the autumn sunshine. They talked in a desultory fashion about the breathtaking view and the warm weather and things in general, until Jarrod asked how her father was doing.

Briana felt herself get defensive, even while she tried not to show it. "He's doing okay."

"Did he enjoy dinner last night? You said you were going to invite him."

"Yes. It was nice."

"Speaking of dinner, Danielle and Sonya Hammond are in town. They've invited us to dinner with them tonight."

She was caught unawares. "Us?"

He shot her a quick look. "Do you have a problem with that?"

"Um—no. I just didn't know you were that close." Danielle and Sonya had lived with Howard Blackstone all these years, so she tended to think of them as Blackstones despite their Hammond surname.

"We're not. That's what Danielle wants to rectify."

Her brow rose. "And you're happy with that?"

He gave a careless shrug and kept his eyes on the road ahead. "They've done nothing to me."

She liked his attitude. "Well then, I'd love to have dinner with you all."

"Good. It's at the casino."

"Oh." She could feel herself grow hot. Perhaps she'd been too hasty in accepting the invitation? The last time she and Jarrod had been at the casino they'd ended up in bed together.

He slanted her a knowing glance, but thankfully they arrived at the crescent-shaped sandy beach with a small pier at one end. The whole coastline was covered in glorious beaches like this, and they decided to go for a walk to the most deserted point before coming back to eat the lunch Jarrod had brought with him.

Being at the beach was such an integral part of the Australian way of life, Briana mused as they walked along the path cutting through the tufts of grass to the sand. She loved Aussie beaches… The smell of the ocean and sand… The sun evaporating the stresses of daily life…

Until Jarrod went to hold her hand, and she snatched it back. "No."

His brow rose. "No?"

"I don't hold hands."

He gave a short laugh. "What do you mean you don't hold hands?"

She moved her shoulders in a shrug. "It's so…"

"Romantic?" he mocked.

"If you like." She hesitated. "My first boyfriend always wanted to hold my hand."

His glance sharpened. "Nothing wrong with that."

"There is when it's *all* the time." She'd been young and wildly in love, but after six months they'd outgrown each other. Or perhaps *she'd* outgrown Derek, she admitted, remembering how his constant handholding had begun to make her feel somehow tied to him. A whole new world was opening up for her as a model, but he'd wanted her to stay the same. At nineteen that was the last thing she wanted.

"How many lovers have you had, Briana?"

She stopped dead. She knew she didn't have to answer but she did. "Three."

He had stopped, too. "Including me?"

She nodded. "Yes, including you."

He studied her face with an enigmatic gaze. "You're not very sexually experienced, are you?"

She stared at him, her heart seeming to open like a flower under the sun. This was another indication that he was beginning to see her as the person she was. "No, I'm not, Jarrod."

His eyes held her captive. "Was your other lover serious?"

He already knew about Patrick, so she knew he meant Derek. "At the time, yes."

"What happened?"

"I was young and so was he. It didn't work out."

Looking back, she realized how very young she'd been, and how ill-prepared for emotional commitment. It had been many years before she'd let herself fall in love again—and with Patrick this time. She winced inwardly. Both affairs had merely proven that love wasn't for her.

Jarrod nodded his head, and in silent agreement they started walking again. "You may not believe this," he said after they'd taken a few steps along the soft sand. "But I'm not a virgin, either."

She had to smile. "I'm totally shocked."

"Yeah, you look it," he teased, then they continued walking in silence for a few more yards, a rare sense of harmony between them. A light breeze from the ocean and the lapping of the gentle waves added to the mood.

A little further on, Jarrod said, "I should have said this long before now, but I'm sorry you lost your mother and sister."

For a moment her throat locked up. "Thank you," she managed. It meant a lot to her for him to say that. Then she cleared her throat. "I just wish things hadn't gone so wrong between her and Matt."

Seconds of silence ticked by and she felt a twinge of disappointment. Had she tested his goodwill to the limit? Was he going to bring up that wall of reserve again?

"I had no idea she had left him," he suddenly admitted. "Not until the plane crash."

Her mind reeled in confusion. "But she and Howard were in the papers for weeks before their deaths."

"And I was in New York working day and night on a case. I barely stopped to eat, let alone read the newspapers."

"But didn't anyone tell you?" she said, walking alongside him.

He slanted a brow at her. "Who?"

"Matt?"

He shook his head with regret. "No. He keeps things to himself."

He wasn't the only one, she mused, glancing at Jarrod's profile as they strolled along the sand. To the outside world they must look like a couple merely enjoying their surroundings. Instead they were opening up to each other in a way they hadn't done before—without recriminations. It was a major breakthrough in their relationship. Perhaps after their affair ended, they could be friends?

Perhaps not.

"Marise wasn't an easy person to love," she admitted. "But I loved her all the same."

He pinned her with another sideways glance. "Of course you did."

She gave a shaky sigh. "She didn't deserve to die."

"No, she didn't."

Briana stopped in her tracks as a sudden overwhelming sense of loss swept over her. How Marise had died would always haunt her. That was the worst part. Knowing that her sister had been floating in a life vest by herself with severe injuries. How dreadfully scared Marise must have felt, realizing she was going to die. She would have given a good fight, but not even when a passing ship had picked her up, had she been able to survive. Briana's only comfort was at least Marise had not died alone. Someone from the ship had been with her. She knew that for a fact.

Jarrod stepped in front of her and with compassion in his eyes, brushed some strands of hair off her cheek. "This is why we should live life to the fullest."

"Yes." For once she wanted to lean into him, against

him, take strength from him. She reached out and placed her hands on his hips, stepping closer, seeing his spurt of surprise and knew this wasn't about sex. This was about comfort, about giving and receiving. And that was something neither of them had tried before.

All at once someone screamed, making them both jump. It only took a split second to take in the situation. A small boy with yellow floaties on his arms had been dragged out into deeper water, his mother was on the shore screaming for help, a small baby in her arms.

"Oh God," Briana muttered, forgetting Jarrod as she immediately started to run toward the water. Others were running, too. She could hear the thud of footsteps in the sand. She wasn't sure what she was going to do. She was a good swimmer but not strong enough to swim that far out. But she couldn't let the little boy drown.

Without warning a man brushed past her as he ran into the shallows, splashing through the water. He was bare-chested but had jeans on. He had dark hair.

Jarrod!

Briana reached the mother just as Jarrod dove into deeper water and began swimming through the small waves. A couple of others were milling around the woman, someone taking the baby out of her arms, someone else offering reassurance.

Briana could only stand and watch as Jarrod sliced through the water, her heart in her mouth. She prayed he reached the child before he was dragged out even further. He was getting closer.

And then sheer fright tore through her. Would Jarrod

have the strength to swim back, let alone with a small child in tow? She didn't think so. It was too far.

She began to shake as time stood still. Yet she was aware of the sounds around her. Of the cold water lapping over her wet sneakers. Of the breeze getting stronger. Of the sun going behind a cloud, making the deeper water look even more menacing.

And she began to pray. If anything happened to Jarrod… If he drowned out there doing this heroic thing… If the ocean took him like it had Marise… She wouldn't be able to bear it.

Please God, don't take the man I love.

Her heart seemed to rise in her chest then tumble headfirst into an emotion she'd been fighting ever since she'd met Jarrod Hammond. She *loved* him. He was what love was all about.

Just at that moment Jarrod reached the boy, and a cheer went up, startling her. And then her prayers were answered when a small boat left the pier at the other end of the bay and headed for them. Another cheer went up, and this time Briana's heart cheered, too.

She still held her breath until Jarrod and the boy were in the boat and then safely ashore. There ensued a ton of commotion as the mother cried and hugged her son, then profusely thanked Jarrod with a kiss and a hug. Someone placed a towel around Jarrod's shoulders, and someone else shook his hand.

Through it all, Briana just stood there, not moving, her eyes going over him like she'd been given the greatest gift on earth.

And she had.

All at once he noticed her standing a few feet away. He walked toward her in his sodden jeans. "Are you okay?" he asked.

No, she would never be the same again.

Her gaze went over his dear, dear features. "Are *you* okay?"

He nodded. "Just a bit wet."

She remembered how she'd felt watching him out there in the ocean. "You could have drowned," she whispered.

"Yeah, well, don't make a fuss," he dismissed in a gruff voice, and turned away to collect his polo shirt and sneakers where he'd dropped them in such a hurry.

It was as if someone had snapped their fingers in front of her and awoken her from a trance. A powerful, overwhelming and crushing sensation went through her. Yes, she loved him, but the last thing she could do was tell him. Nothing had changed on his part. He'd warned her at the beginning not to expect anything more than a temporary relationship. She wouldn't go back on her word.

Besides, she had to be realistic. There were too many other things between them. Marise…Matt…her father… Oh Lord, if she told him about her father's embezzlement what would he do? As a lawyer, would he be obligated to tell the police if he knew a wrongdoing had been committed? She couldn't even tell him that Patrick was blackmailing her for fear of it all coming out in the open.

After the commotion died down, Briana suggested they leave. Though the journey back was quiet, she was inwardly screaming to get some time to herself. Jarrod needed to get out of his wet things and take a shower, only she didn't want to join him. Not when her love for him was pumping through her body…through her heart. Not when she somehow had to keep up all pretences until she could leave next week. Oh God, it was going to be a long, long week. Yet in some ways not long enough.

She was rather distant when they arrived back at her apartment building. "Please don't come up. You need to go home and change."

He stared hard, his forehead creased in a frown. "What's the matter? You've been quiet ever since I helped save the boy."

She couldn't let him dismiss his actions so easily. "You didn't just *help,* Jarrod. You saved his life."

"I couldn't let him drown."

Love swelled inside her. "I know you couldn't." She leaned over and kissed him softly on the lips. "You're a fine man, Jarrod Hammond," she murmured, pulling back. Her heart wobbled with love and a warning quickly filled her. "I just need to be alone for a little while."

His gaze softened with surprising tenderness. "It's because of Marise, isn't it? Seeing me out there in the water reminded you of how she died."

She nodded, gratefully grabbing at the suggestion, though it was true anyway.

"I understand," he said, and skimmed his lips over hers. "Do you still want to come to dinner tonight?"

The casino! She'd forgotten about that for a moment. It was going to be hard returning to the scene of their first time together, knowing she loved him. But she'd still go to support Jarrod, whether he wanted that support or not. She could do it. After all, if he had drowned today….

"Yes," she whispered, then got out of the car, hearing his comment about picking her up at seven. She nodded and said she'd be ready. She just hoped that emotionally, she would be.

Eight

"Hello, Sonya," Jarrod said as they reached the table in the middle of the luxurious casino restaurant, and Briana watched as Sonya lifted her elegant head from the menu, her eyes widening.

In her late forties, Sonya always reminded Briana of a stunning and graceful queen. Queen Sonya. Yes, she certainly seemed to be the queen of the Blackstone family, and deservedly so. The woman had lived at Howard's mansion since her sister's suicide nearly thirty years ago, raising Kim and Ryan along with her own daughter, Danielle. Remembering that, Briana immediately felt a bond with her. Sonya had lost a sister, just like she had.

"Jarrod! Oh my God! What are you doing here? What a coincidence," Sonya said with delighted surprise.

Jarrod kissed her cheek. "No coincidence," he said

as a small smile tugged the corners of his firm mouth. Then he kissed Danielle's cheek. "Danielle planned it."

Sonya swung toward her daughter. "Danielle!"

"I thought it would be a nice surprise, Mum," Danielle said with a wide smile, her golden eyes shining with pleasure, her charm a part of her beauty.

"Oh, it is. It is. It's a lovely surprise," Sonya agreed, her gaze on Jarrod, who looked handsome and debonair in a dark suit. Then Sonya's gaze fell on Briana. "And, Briana, how nice to see you again," she said warmly, and Briana wondered how she'd ever thought this woman was coolly reserved.

"It's nice to see you, too, Sonya." Briana then smiled at Danielle, whose copper-colored curls seemed to want to burst out from their bun. "You, too, Danielle."

"Please. Call me Dani."

Sonya rolled her eyes. "I give my daughter such a beautiful name and she chops it in half." She waved a hand at the two empty chairs on the other side of the table. "Please. Sit down."

Briana thanked Jarrod as he held out her chair for her.

"Well, this *is* nice," Sonya said, glowing with enjoyment. "It's just so good to have you here, Jarrod. We didn't get to talk much at the jewelry launch a few weeks ago, nor at Kim's wedding. I was hoping to catch you afterward but what with all the media swarming around afterward, I decided to go straight home."

"I left a bit early anyway," Jarrod said, confirming Briana's suspicions.

"Wise man." Sonya took a moment to smile at

Briana. "And you looked so gorgeous at the jewelry launch, Briana. I was wishing that was me up there."

"Easily," Briana said, not fawning, merely stating the truth. "But thank you. It all went very well."

The evening went well, too…until Briana's gaze caught Jarrod's by accident and everything came tumbling back. Until now she hadn't let herself think about being here, but returning to "the scene of the crime", the sounds of the casino, the scents of perfume and aftershave, of food, the gleam in Jarrod's eyes, reminded her what they had done together here in one of the casino suites—all for the sake of a million dollars.

And now she loved him.

And he could have died today.

Quickly she lowered her lashes, breaking the invisible thread between them. He may be getting a kick out of revisiting all this, but she wasn't. She would never be able to come into this place again without thinking of the man she loved. She doubted she'd ever be able to go to the beach now without thinking of him either. He would always be a part of her now. And a part of her memories.

Sonya's question broke into her thoughts. "How is your father, Jarrod?" she said casually, but they all knew her interest was more than casual about her brother—the brother she hadn't spoken to for almost thirty years.

For the first time tonight, Jarrod's face became shuttered. "As well as can be expected," he said smoothly, without any hint of the anguish that had passed between their families.

"I was praying Oliver would be up and about by now."

"So were we. But the stroke has taken its toll, I'm afraid."

"Yes, I know. I spoke to Katherine a few months ago," Sonya said, obviously surprising the others. "She's not as hopeful of a full recovery as she was before." She blinked rapidly, as if to stop sudden tears. "It *has* been five years after all."

"These things can take longer than we expect, Sonya," he said, making Briana wonder if in addition to his father's health he meant family issues, as well.

Briana could only think how much stood between these two families. Sonya and Dani were Hammonds yet they'd been shunned by Sonya's brother, Oliver, who was Jarrod's father. Families needed to work things out. How she wished she had her mother back to talk to. And Marise. She'd make it work with her sister if she had another chance, she told herself, despair cutting the air from her lungs.

"Yes, they do take time," the older woman agreed softly, a hopeful looking crossing her face.

An awkward silence ensued but fortunately their first course arrived.

"I must say," Dani began as she picked up her fork, "you have some great shopping here in Melbourne. We were going to come down last weekend, only Mum didn't want to fight the crowds from the Grand Prix."

Sonya shuddered. "I love Melbourne, but car racing is not my thing. Mind you, Kim and Ric were here. Ryan and Jessica, too. They were hosting a corporate box." She paused as she glanced casually at Jarrod. "They said they saw you, Jarrod."

"Briefly."

A moment crept by.

"I was there, too," Briana said to ease the silence. "It was great catching up with them all. Jessica is blooming in her pregnancy."

Sonya sighed. "I'm so grateful they're happy." She glanced across at her daughter with a loving smile. "Children are such a blessing."

Dani pointed a fork at her. "That's not what you said when I told you I was going back to Port Douglas."

Sonya smiled at Jarrod and Briana. "On the other hand—"

"Mother!" Dani laughingly joked.

"As I said, a blessing—" She paused. "In disguise."

Everyone laughed, and then continued eating.

"So, Dani," Jarrod said when there was a lull in conversation. "You like Port Douglas, do you?"

Her eyes lit up. "I love it."

Briana was impressed by Dani's considerable talent. "How is your shop going up there? I loved those pieces you designed for the jewelry launch."

Dani looked thoroughly delighted. "Thank you. I've got so many clients out of that. I've almost paid back Howard's estate the money he loaned me to start the business."

"You design jewelry?" Jarrod said, obviously not knowing. "You must be very good if Howard lent you money."

Dani's chin lifted in the air. "No, Howard Blackstone is *not* my father," she said, a feistiness entering her tone.

"Danielle!" Sonya said, scolding her daughter.

Dani immediately grimaced. "I'm sorry. I'm just so used to everyone thinking Howard is my father that I wanted to set the record straight." She looked across the table at Jarrod. "It's important to me that you know the truth, Jarrod. I mean, I'm grateful to Howard and I was fond of him—but I'm a Hammond, as well."

Jarrod looked directly at his cousin. "Dani, I never did believe any of that crap in the newspaper."

Sonya cleared her throat. "Thank you, Jarrod. This means a lot to me." She reached out and squeezed Dani's hand. "To us."

"Yes," Dani added, her eyes a little watery. "Thank you."

Briana could have kissed Jarrod. She knew how much his family hated Howard Blackstone, how much he disliked the man himself, yet he was able to stand back from that now and realize these two people weren't to blame. Her love for him deepened.

"I once did a magazine shoot in Port Douglas, Dani," Briana said, giving them a moment to recover. "It's beautiful, and you certainly get some pretty famous people up there. I saw a couple of movie stars from the States."

Dani waved her hand in a dismissive gesture. "That's nothing compared to all the hoopla with the Governor-General coming up there on ANZAC Day for a commemoration. You should see those preparations."

Suddenly there was a clang of cutlery and everyone

looked at Sonya, who had dropped her fork on her plate. She'd turned as white as a sheet and had a faint sheen of perspiration on her upper lip.

"Mum?" Dani said, quickly leaning toward her mother. "What's the matter?"

Sonya went to say something, swallowed, then began again. "Um—I'm fine, darling. I just came over cold and clammy all of a sudden." She dabbed at her top lip with a napkin but she still looked white.

"But I wasn't feeling the best before we came," she added, surprising Briana because she'd thought Sonya was a picture of health. Then she looked at Jarrod. "I hope you don't mind, but I think I may need to go and lie down."

"Of course I don't mind." Jarrod got to his feet. "I'll take you to your room."

Sonya waved him back in his seat. "No. Dani and I will manage."

"Come on, Mum. Let's get you up to our suite. I want to get the doctor to look you over." As Dani started to lead her away she promised Jarrod she'd call.

After they left, Briana looked at Jarrod worriedly. "I hope it's nothing too serious."

He'd been frowning, but his forehead cleared. "It's probably just a stomach bug."

"But it did come out of the blue, didn't it?" Briana said, still concerned. "It was like she had a shock, though I guess a stomach bug has the same symptoms." She dismissed her own thought. "Oh well. No matter. As long as she recovers."

"Hmm. I wonder if Sonya planned this," Jarrod said

later. "It's a novel way of getting out of paying the bill, don't you think?"

"Oh, she wouldn't—" Briana began, then saw the twinkle in his eye. "I'm sure you can afford it."

"I guess it's better than the million dollars I spent here last time," he said, more teasing than not.

But she didn't find it funny. She felt hurt. "That's not very gentlemanly of you to bring that up."

His amusement disappeared. "Hey, it's not like you didn't take the money."

Oh, how she wished she could tell him the truth. Things might be different for them. But she had her father to think about first. Herself second. She could never enjoy any happiness with Jarrod at her father's expense. If indeed there was any happiness to be had.

He tilted his head and considered her. "Would you have slept with me without the money, Briana?"

"No."

"Sure?" he asked silkily.

Her heart trembled. "I don't deny I was attracted to you, but no, I wouldn't have taken it further without the money." She would never have let herself be put in the position to sleep with him.

His mouth tightened. "Some things can't be ignored, Briana. And our attraction was one of them. I think you would have."

"Then we'll have to agree to disagree," she said sweetly, but her heart was sinking in her chest. If he knew she loved him… If he knew he held her heart in his hands…

"How about I give you another million dollars to come up to a suite with me?"

The thought staggered her. "Don't be silly."

His eyebrow rose. "So you don't want the money? That doesn't add up. You took a million dollars the first time but you won't take another million now."

"Perhaps I'm not as greedy as you think," she said, encouraging him to think that way about her. After everything, if he thought good about her, then she'd be happy.

For a moment he studied her intently. "Perhaps not."

She ignored a flash of relief. "Jarrod, it's been a long day. Would you mind taking me home? I'm starting to get a headache." She saw his instant concern. "No, nothing like Sonya just had." Her own headache was tension, she was sure. From loving a man who didn't love her, nor would he ever *want* to love her.

Once back at her building she turned to him in the car. "Do you mind if you don't come up tonight?" This was the second time today she'd said the same thing.

The streetlight showed his glance sharpen. "I mind, but if that's the way you feel I won't push myself on you."

"Thank you."

"But I insist on walking you to your door." And he did. Once there, he kissed her goodnight, but it was a brief kiss. "I'll call you later in the week."

"Okay." She breathed easier. She'd asked for time to herself and he was giving her more than enough.

"Miss me," he said, and headed back to the elevator.

It wasn't a suggestion.

She would take it to heart.

* * *

The next morning when her doorbell rang, Briana's pulse started racing. Jarrod! He wasn't waiting to phone her. He wanted to see her now. Today. It made her heart flutter even as she told herself not to care.

But when she opened the door, it was to find a stranger there. A very handsome and impeccably dressed stranger.

"Briana, hello. I'm Quinn Everard."

Her forehead cleared. She easily recognized the smooth, strong voice that would put more than a little spring in a woman's step. Not her step, of course. Jarrod was the only man to make her heart leap.

"Can I come in?"

"What? I'm sorry. Yes, please do come in." She stepped back to let him pass.

"I apologize for dropping by like this," he said as he stepped into her apartment.

She suddenly realized something. "Sorry if I sound confused, but I'm not sure how you got past the doorman."

"There was no one at the front desk, so I just followed another lady into the building."

"Oh—well, I'm glad I'm not being stalked." She smiled to take the sting out of her words, but this time she did intend to speak to the building manager about this. As a high-profile person, she was a prime target for anyone with a grudge or a fixation. The various letters sent to her agent over the years assured her of that.

He gave a slow smile that reminded her of Jarrod. "I hope I don't look the type to cause trouble."

"Not at all. Have a seat. Would you like a cup of coffee?"

"No, thanks." He sat down on the edge of the sofa, resting his elbows on his thighs. "I'm here to tell you about the diamonds you wanted valued."

"You didn't need to come all this way. You could have—"

"Have you ever heard of the Blackstone Rose necklace?" he cut across her.

She lowered herself down on the sofa opposite him. "The Blackstone Rose necklace?" she asked, thinking. Then her face cleared. "Oh yes. There was a vague reference to it in the papers recently."

"That's right. It was a necklace that went missing nearly thirty years ago. It belonged to Ursula Blackstone, Howard's wife, who died just after the necklace went missing."

"She committed suicide, didn't she?" Her brow crinkled. "But what has this to do with the diamonds Marise put in my safe?"

Seconds crept by. An excited light came into his eyes, an aura about him that held her full attention now. "Marise's diamonds belonged to the Blackstone Rose necklace."

Briana's head reeled. "What? But I don't understand. How could Marise have diamonds belonging to a necklace missing almost thirty years?"

"That's what I'd like to know."

What he was suggesting took a moment to sink in.

Then she inhaled sharply. "You don't think I had anything to do with this, do you?"

"Relax, Briana. I don't think you're involved," he assured her. "But I *am* hoping you might inadvertently know something. That's why I wanted to talk to you face-to-face."

She expelled a breath. "I'm happy to tell you what I can, but I just don't know that much."

He slowly nodded, then gave her an encouraging smile. "How about I start at the beginning and we'll see if anything rings a bell?"

She cleared her throat. "Fine."

"Okay. The story goes that in 1970 Ursula's father, Jeb Hammond, was fossicking in the Outback when he found a massive pink diamond that was a rare and extremely valuable find. Jeb called it the Heart of the Outback." He paused to let this sink in. "A few years later he gifted it to Ursula on the birth of his first grandson, then Howard had it turned into the Blackstone Rose necklace."

Her forehead creased as fragments of past information flashed through her mind. "That was the grandson who was kidnapped, wasn't it?"

Quinn's mouth flattened in a grim line. "Yes. James was two years old when he was abducted. But Howard always believed his son was alive, and now it looks like he may have been right."

"Yes, so I'd heard." She remembered thinking how Jarrod may have been the missing heir, and his derision when she'd mentioned it to him.

"Ursula never recovered from losing her son. As you

know, she had two more children, Kimberley and Ryan, but she suffered badly from post-natal depression after Ryan's birth. Eventually she walked into the ocean and committed suicide."

Briana sighed. "Such a tragedy," she murmured.

"But I digress," Quinn said. "The necklace. It was at Ursula's thirtieth birthday that it disappeared from around her neck. Apparently she was quite drunk and fell into the swimming pool. Some of the guests helped her to her room, but by this time the necklace was missing and Howard accused her brother, Oliver, of stealing it." Quinn's eyes hardened. "Of course, Howard also accused Oliver of arranging the kidnapping of James, a claim Oliver vehemently denied, and the brothers-in-law never spoke to each other again. Not that I blame Oliver," he said, a bitter twist to his lips that made her ask a question before she could stop herself.

"You didn't like Howard?"

His jaw clenched. "Howard Blackstone was vindictive and manipulative and very good at using people and destroying them." His face closed up even more. "It's personal."

She took the hint. "So, the necklace was never found?"

"No. And the insurance company refused to pay out because of a loophole in the policy wording."

"And there were never any leads?" she asked.

He shook his head. "Despite exhaustive investigations, no one was ever charged with the theft. Howard continued to blame Oliver."

Briana felt so sorry for Jarrod's father. Oliver had

more than enough justification to cut ties with Howard, though she didn't believe Oliver should have cut Sonya out of his life. A sister was for life.

And speaking of sisters… "Where does Marise come into all this?"

"I don't know," he said. "Perhaps you could start by telling me what she said about the diamonds when she put them in your safe."

"She didn't say much at all, I'm afraid."

"Tell me anyway."

Briana thought back. It hurt to picture the scene but it had to be done. "We were in Sydney for my mother's funeral and—" She stopped, then cleared her throat. "Marise, my father and I were staying at my Sydney apartment, which is paid for by Blackstone's as I do a lot of engagements in Sydney. I remember Marise asking if she could have the combination to my wall safe so she could keep some jewelry in there. Naturally I gave it to her." She took a shuddering breath. "Then after our mother's funeral, I came back here to Melbourne with my father. I was grieving, and trying to keep an eye on him, but I was also trying to fulfill my pre-Christmas engagements. It's all just a blur now."

"I understand," he said, his voice sympathetic.

"Then I started hearing about Marise and Howard and—" She swallowed hard. "I honestly don't know what to believe about them. All I know is that just before I went to Howard's funeral I remembered the jewelry in the safe. I checked and there were the diamonds, so I phoned Matt to tell him I had some jewelry belonging to Marise, but he didn't want to know." She winced, then, "So I mentioned it to Jessica and she gave me your name." She lifted her shoulders in a faint shrug. "Sorry, I'm not much help."

"That's okay. You're doing fine." His eyes took on an alert look. "Did you tell Matt they were pink diamonds?"

She thought back. "No. I just said jewelry. Why?"

He shrugged. "No reason. Was there anything else in the safe?"

"Only a few bits and pieces of my own jewelry." Something occurred to her and her eyes widened. "Oh God, could Howard have given them to her, do you think?"

Quinn scowled. "I don't know, Briana. It would mean Howard either had the necklace all along, or came into it again without telling anyone. And why give it to Marise? Unless—" His eyes flickered away then back to her.

"Unless she was his mistress," Briana said what he'd been too polite to say. "I'm afraid I can't answer that question. I just don't know why Marise was with Howard. I'm not sure we'll ever find out."

"You're probably right."

Her brow furrowed. "What happens with the diamonds now?"

"They should go to the Blackstone lawyers."

She nodded. "Of course. Would you be able to give them to the lawyers on my behalf?"

"Absolutely." He stood up. "I'm returning to Sydney this afternoon and I'll hand deliver them myself as soon as I can."

"Thank you," she said with relief. "Just do whatever

you have to do to make sure they are returned to their rightful owner."

"I will."

She didn't want the responsibility of such valuable items in her care now. God, when she thought about what she'd unwittingly had in her possession… And Matt, he'd be kicking himself for not taking them back. Not that he would have kept them once he found out they belonged to the Blackstones.

Quinn left not long after that, and Briana sat on the sofa again, thinking. How on earth had Marise come by the diamonds? And what had she been planning on doing with them? Not to mention, who had stolen the necklace in the first place?

At the thought, she felt a sudden chill. Would everyone think *she* was involved somehow? After all, it had been her sister with the diamonds, and they'd been in her safe.

What sort of person would Jarrod think she was? She'd taken a million dollars off him, and now she had the stones in her possession. She knew his opinion of her had risen lately, but now, would this set it back? More than likely, she thought with despair.

Oh Marise, she whispered to herself, what have you done?

The only good thing in all this was that the diamonds would now be returned to their rightful owner. More than likely Kim, as the eldest. And Kim would believe her, she was sure. She just hoped this didn't put her contract into question with the other powers-that-be at Blackstone's.

Nine

Time was running out, and Briana was sick at heart for the rest of the day. She felt guilty for keeping the news of the diamonds from Jarrod, yet next week her relationship with him would be over and she'd be on her way to Hong Kong anyway. With Patrick. So why bother telling Jarrod about the diamonds? Why spoil their last week together? Every moment together was precious. She couldn't think beyond that.

The only good news was when her father called and said he'd managed to put the money back in Howard's account. The relief she felt was tremendous. Her father was still guilty of embezzlement but at least now no one could accuse him of keeping the money for himself.

So for her, it was all worthwhile. Sleeping with

Jarrod, spending time in his company. Oh yes, very worthwhile. If heartbreaking now.

Over the next few days, Briana tried to forget about the diamonds while she concentrated on preparing for her overseas assignment. Jarrod had called once or twice, but he was busy with a heavy case. She understood but she missed him. And it made time tick even more loudly in her ears.

And then two days later he took her out to dinner. It was a warm March evening and daylight saving time didn't finish until the end of the month, so it should have been pleasant eating and watching the sun set over the city. Briana spent most of her time trying to act normal, but the pink diamonds from the necklace were at the back of her mind. At the front was the thought of heading to Hong Kong next week and leaving Jarrod.

They ended up back at her apartment where she went into his arms and let him make love to her. Yet no matter that she badly wanted to show him how much she loved him, she still had to restrain herself, knowing that if she gave him her all, she might well fall apart right there and then.

Afterward, she lay in the crook of his arm, a slither of moonlight falling over them. If she could just commit this moment to memory… His masculine scent… The smoothness of his skin… The springy feel of chest hair beneath her palm…

"Is everything okay?" he said, his deep voice rumbling in her ear, cutting across her thoughts.

She mentally pulled herself together. "Why wouldn't it be?"

"You tell me."

She hardly dared breathe. "I don't know what you mean."

"You were distracted tonight."

She lifted one bare shoulder in a shrug. "I've got a lot on my mind."

"Like?"

She hesitated. "I'm leaving for Hong Kong next week," she pointed out, wanting to remind him that this would all end soon. She didn't fool herself that the end of their relationship would impact him like it did her, but it would've been nice to know he'd feel a little sad about them going their separate ways.

He tensed. "So that's next week then?" he said casually, as if he hadn't realized, though she knew he must. Jarrod never forgot a thing.

"Yes. The month will be up then."

A lengthy silence followed, then all at once he gently moved her off him and pushed himself out of bed. "I'd better go home. I have an early appointment."

So much for her thinking he might care, she thought with despair as he dressed in the dark. His movements weren't hurried, yet she had the feeling he couldn't wait to get away from her. He probably couldn't wait to get rid of her for good now.

Then he kissed her and left.

It was a long time before she fell asleep after that.

The last person she wanted to see the next day at a

fashion parade was Patrick. The Chadstone Shopping Center might be one of the biggest in the southern hemisphere but it wasn't big enough to get away from this man.

"So, sweetheart," he said, standing in the doorway with a smirk as he watched her change into another outfit. "You're all ready for our trip next week I hope?"

"Yes," she all but growled at him.

He lifted an eyebrow. "Going to give lover boy the flick this weekend, are you?"

"That's none of your business."

"Yes, it is. I don't want him coming after you and spoiling things on the shoot for me." His eyes narrowed. "You make it clear to him that it's over, right?"

She considered him with distaste. "I don't know what I ever saw in you, Patrick."

His lips twisted in a cynical smile. "Do you think I care?"

"No. You care about no one but yourself."

"I'm glad you realize that."

She watched him turn and walk away like he didn't have a care in the world. It was all an act. He cared what people thought of him, but only for his own advantage.

And she knew one thing. If Patrick had known about the pink diamonds, he would have sold them on the black market, and he wouldn't have cared less. Of that she was certain.

Jarrod didn't see Briana again until Saturday. Until then he'd stayed away through choice. He was trying to wean himself off her. She'd begun to play a significant part in his life, and he wasn't happy about it. This was only supposed to be a fling with a beautiful model. He should have worked her out of his system by now. So why hadn't he?

Dammit, he couldn't deny the way his gut had knotted the other night in bed when she'd mentioned leaving. The thought of her going away for two weeks made him ache to hold her in his arms, but it was more than that. It was knowing once she left it would be the end for them.

Hell, he had to have some integrity. He'd offered her money, she'd taken it, they'd made an agreement. And now that agreement was coming to an end. He'd go his way and she'd go hers. Intimate strangers.

And then on Saturday morning his brother called him, and everything Jarrod had previously believed about Briana rose up and punched him the gut, making that knot unravel pretty damn quickly.

"I hope you're sitting down for this, Jarrod," Matt said, an excited note in his voice that immediately caught Jarrod's attention. "Quinn Everard has found four of the five pink diamonds from the Blackstone Rose necklace."

"You're kidding," Jarrod said, leaning back against the kitchen counter. He'd grown up hearing all about the missing necklace and all the heartache it had caused. "Dad must be thrilled."

"He is. It's given him a real boost." There was a slight hesitation. "There's something else. Briana had them."

Jarrod straightened. "What!"

"Quinn said Briana asked him to value them."

Jarrod swore. "Go on."

"Apparently Marise asked if she could keep some jewelry in Briana's wall safe in her Sydney apartment, so Briana gave her the combination. It wasn't until just before Howard's funeral that Briana remembered, and that's when she found the diamonds." Matt paused. "She told me, you know. She said she had some jewelry of Marise's and I told her to keep the damn lot." He cursed at himself. "How the hell was I supposed to know they were diamonds belonging to the necklace?"

Jarrod tried to take it all in. "But what was Marise doing with them? And why the hell didn't Briana at least mention them to me?"

"Who knew why Marise did anything," Matt said bitterly, reminding Jarrod that good news or not about the diamonds, this was going to stir up Matt's ill-feelings again for his late wife. Then, "I hear you've been seeing Briana."

"Yes," Jarrod said tightly.

"Quinn said she had no idea what the diamonds were," Matt pointed out, obviously still having a soft spot for Briana, despite her being Marise's sister.

Jarrod's jaw clenched and his hand tightened around the telephone. "She still should have mentioned them."

Matt didn't speak for a few seconds. "Here's something else that's strange. I heard a recent rumor on the underground grapevine. It was about the Davenports. Apparently, long ago the Davenport name was mentioned in connection to the missing necklace." He paused significantly. "*Before* Marise and Briana were born."

A second shock wave rocked through Jarrod. He tried to take it all in. "How substantial is the rumor?"

"The diamonds pretty much confirm it."

Jarrod expelled a breath. "This is too damn incredible."

Matt waited a moment before asking, "What are you going to do?"

He stiffened. "Speak to Briana," he said, his voice holding an ominous quality.

"Let me know what develops. I've asked Quinn to look for the fifth diamond, but if she knows anything at all, I want to hear about it." His unspoken words said "for Oliver Hammond's sake."

Jarrod hung up the phone and stood there letting it all sink in. He felt gutted. Briana had kept all this from him. It made him wonder what the hell else she was hiding.

Briana started frowning as soon as she heard the buzzer sound on Saturday morning. When she answered, it was to find Jarrod standing there. "You're early for our lunch date."

"I know," he snarled at her as he stepped past her into the living room.

He looked…odd. "What's going on?"

His gaze seared her. "Perhaps I should be asking *you* that."

Her misgivings increased by the moment as she slowly closed the door and turned to face him. The distance was more than the length of the room between them. "What do you mean?"

"The diamonds, Briana."

Her frown deepened. "Diamonds?"

"Pink ones," he drawled with deceptive mildness. "From the Blackstone Rose necklace."

Her forehead cleared, and just as quickly her heart sank. "But how do you—"

"Matt told me."

"Matt?" She shook her head, trying to make sense of what Jarrod was saying.

"The diamonds belong to him now."

Shock ran through her. "But how? Why?" Dear God, she didn't understand what this was all about. And Jarrod obviously blamed her already without a fair hearing.

"Marise was left the Blackstone jewelry collection, remember? On her death, it all went to her husband." He paused. "Matt."

"But I thought the Blackstone Rose diamonds would belong to the Blackstones."

"Howard obviously thought differently. He bequeathed *all* the jewelry to Marise."

"But surely not the Blackstone Rose?" She'd known about the jewelry going to Marise of course, but this was different. This was the Blackstone Rose necklace, for heaven's sake. Howard couldn't have known it was going to resurface, and even if he had, why leave it to Marise in his will?

She let out a shaky breath. "I still don't understand."

"Join the club," he said scathingly.

She ignored that, not sure if it was meant for her or himself. Probably both. "Is Matt going to give it back to the Blackstones?"

Jarrod snorted with derision. "I doubt it. My father will be very pleased to have the diamonds back where they belong—with the Hammond family. It should never have gone to Howard in the first place. The only reason Howard married Ursula was to get his hands on the Heart of the Outback diamond."

"You can't know that."

"I know Howard."

She tilted her head at him. "I didn't realize you were quite so…involved with the family feud between the Blackstones and the Hammonds."

"I'm a Hammond. I'm involved," he snapped.

She realized she'd touched a nerve about his adoption.

He pinned her with his eyes. "Why didn't you tell me about the diamonds, Briana?"

Suddenly she felt a chill. This was it. "I didn't think they were important."

"Oh come on! You must have known Marise had put them in the safe and what they were."

"At the time I knew she put some jewelry in the safe. That's all." Her eyes searched his, and hurt ripped at her insides. "You don't believe me, do you?"

"No," he freely admitted. "Not when there's a Davenport connection to the stolen necklace all those years ago."

Her stomach lurched. "What?"

"Matt learned on the underground grapevine today that the Davenport name was linked to the missing necklace almost thirty years ago."

She shook her head. "No way. Besides, neither Marise nor I were even born then."

"No, but your parents were."

His words hung in the air. She swallowed a lump in her throat. "You can't believe—"

"That your parents stole the necklace, left Howard's employ, moved to Melbourne where they sold one of the diamonds, and in later years told you and Marise all about it? Does it sound so far-fetched, considering the circumstances?"

She stared aghast. "I don't believe I'm hearing this."

"Your parents were pretty cushy with Howard at one time."

Panic flared. She didn't want Jarrod linking her father and Howard. "So?"

One dark eyebrow rose upward. "So you do know about their past association with Howard?"

"If you mean, do I know that Howard fired my mother when she got pregnant with Marise, then yes, I know." Briana still couldn't understand it but she remembered her mother saying those had been the times back then. Howard wouldn't get away with it these days.

"How did Marise come by the diamonds then?" he shot at her. "And why didn't you tell me about them?"

She didn't appreciate his interrogation. "I don't know why Marise had them. And I've already told you I didn't know what the diamonds were. If I did, why would I get them appraised and risk being discovered? Why would I have told Quinn to give them back to their rightful owner?"

"To protect your family."

She stiffened. "What do you mean?"

"You know your parents stole the necklace. You know Marise, as the eldest daughter, had been given the remaining diamonds. And you thought pretending ignorance was the best way of clearing their names."

His words distressed her. How could he think all that? "You've got it all wrong, Jarrod. Very wrong."

"I want to speak to your father."

She sucked in a sharp breath. "Wh-what?"

"I said I want to speak to Ray. I want to hear what he has to say about all this."

Anxiety twisted inside her. "But you can't—I won't—"

"Feeling guilty?" he growled.

"No." Yes, because of the money.

He stared hard. "Then you won't have a problem if I speak to him."

Somehow she had to get through to him. "Look, he's been through so much. His lost his wife and one of his daughters and now you're accusing him of God knows what. Leave him alone. Please, Jarrod."

His face remained rigid. "I'm going to speak to him no matter what you say."

Begging hadn't worked, so she forced herself to look at him with steely-eyed determination. "I'll never forgive you if you do."

He didn't even flinch. "I'll never forgive myself if I don't."

She realized he was deadly serious. He wasn't going

to be swayed. He would talk to her father with or without her. And if her father wasn't prepared…

With a supreme effort, she squared her shoulders and gave in. "I'll come with you."

Ten

"Ray, we need to talk," Jarrod said as soon as her father opened his front door.

"It's okay, Dad," Briana blurted so he would know it wasn't about the money. Despite it, she saw the flicker of apprehension in her father's eyes and prayed that Jarrod would think it was merely confusion.

Her father stepped back. "You'd better come in," he said with a calmness he must not be feeling. Then once they were all in the living room and Jarrod refused the invitation to sit down with a shake of his head, Ray stood, too. "So, what is it we need to talk about, Jarrod?"

"It's about those diamonds, Dad," Briana said, and received a dark look from Jarrod, but she didn't want her father getting mixed up and inadvertently saying anything he shouldn't.

"Diamonds?"

"You know the ones, Dad," she continued. "I told you about them. Remember those four pink diamonds I found in my safe?"

Ray frowned. "Yes, but—"

"They belong to the Blackstone Rose necklace," Jarrod said, obviously deciding it was time to take control.

Ray blinked. "What?"

"Dad, those four pink diamonds Marise put in my safe belonged to the missing necklace," Briana said gently. She understood his confusion only too well. "Do you know why she would have had them in the first place?"

Ray shook his graying head. "No." Then he seemed to realize they were waiting for more information. "Honey, your sister was a law unto herself. She was my daughter but she did what she wanted, no matter who she hurt, may she rest in peace," he said, his voice choking a little on the last sentence.

Briana blinked back sudden tears as a moment crept by. Yes, that had been Marise.

"Ray," Jarrod began, his voice quiet but unwavering. "You and your wife used to work for Howard Blackstone, didn't you?"

"Yes. And I remember when the necklace went missing."

"It was never recovered."

"Not as far as I know." All at once her father's shoulders tensed. "What are you implying?"

"Ray, did you steal the necklace?"

"What the hell!"

"Jarrod," Briana warned at the same time. She didn't like Jarrod playing the lawyer with her father.

"Did you steal the Blackstone Rose necklace?" Jarrod demanded, ignoring her.

"No!"

"Then how did Marise come by it?"

Ray shot him a hostile glare. "Perhaps Howard gave it to her."

"If it had been recovered earlier, Howard wouldn't have been able to keep that to himself." He gave a cynical twist to his lips. "No, I don't think Howard gave it to Marise at all."

Ray shrugged his shoulders. "Then I'm afraid I can't help you."

"Barbara—"

"I can assure you my wife didn't steal it either." If her father's glare was hostile before, it was doubly hostile now.

Jarrod stood his ground. "Ray, look. Try and step back from this for a minute. It's a possibility, isn't it?"

"Anything's a possibility," her father snapped.

Briana had had enough. "Dad, what Jarrod is getting at is that you and Mum stole the necklace, then we moved here to get away with it, that you gave it to Marise as the elder daughter, and that I got the diamonds valued to put everyone off the scent."

"But—but—that's preposterous!" Ray exclaimed.

"Really?" Jarrod said. "Then the rumor Matt heard is obviously wrong."

Her father's forehead creased. "Rumor?"

"From the underground grapevine. They're saying there's a Davenport connection to the missing necklace."

"Good Lord!" Her father looked totally confused. "I don't understand. How can they say that?" He shook his head. "Why would someone jump to such a conclusion?"

"Just like *you're* doing now," Briana said pointedly to Jarrod.

Jarrod ignored her. "I could accept that was the case *if* it had been an open rumor, but for it to be an underground one it must be pretty well substantiated." He watched the older man carefully. "The interesting thing is that only four diamonds were recovered and there were five. One is still missing. Matt believes it's something to do with your family, and seeing that Briana and Marise weren't even born when the necklace was stolen, we can only assume you or your wife must have appropriated it."

"Jarrod, will you stop this!" Briana exclaimed. "Dad knows nothing about it."

Amazingly, Jarrod stood his ground. "I think he does."

"What gives you the right to come in here and—"

"I took it," Ray cut across her.

Briana gasped. "What?"

"I said I took the necklace."

"Dad, no!"

Jarrod's expression became thoughtful. "Then where is the other pink diamond?"

"I—um—sold it."

"To whom?"

"I—um—can't say. It's confidential."

"It was stolen. It can't be confidential." Jarrod stared

hard. "I don't think you're telling the truth, Ray. I think your wife stole the necklace." He paused. "Am I right?"

Ray held his gaze. Tension filled the air. Then he took two steps to the sofa and sank down on it. "Yes," he whispered.

Briana's mind spun. This wasn't true. It couldn't be. Her mother wouldn't do such a thing. "No, you're wrong. You're—"

Ray looked up. "Sweetheart, I'm sorry, but she *must* have stolen it."

Briana frowned. "How do you know that?"

"Because *I* didn't."

Tears pricked at her blue eyes. "Oh, Dad, don't be silly. Just because you didn't take it doesn't mean Mum *did.*" She spun toward Jarrod. "This is all your fault. You're browbeating him into a confession so that he can keep my mother's good name."

"Briana, shhh," her father said. "Jarrod's just trying to get to the truth."

"For what?" she choked. "To prove some stupid rumor? There's no evidence, Dad. None at all. Jarrod is just—" All at once she noticed her father's dismayed expression. "Dad, are you all right? Dad, what is it?"

"Oh God. I've just remembered something. Your mother wanted you and your sister to go to a private school. We didn't have the money but then a spinster aunt left her a legacy—quite a substantial amount—and your mother put it into an account for your schooling."

Briana's heart jolted. "What are you saying? That there was no spinster aunt?"

"That's exactly what I'm saying."

"But Mum would never—"

"Honey, I loved your mother dearly, but she was never quite the same after Howard fired her. She rarely mentioned him but I always had the impression she had never forgiven him, and rightly so." His mouth turned grim. "I know she was upset at first when Marise went to work for him, but then she seemed to accept it. And the same thing happened when you were given the Blackstone contract, though I know she didn't let on to any of us."

Briana was trying to take all this in. Her mother…her beloved mother…

Jarrod's voice cut across her thoughts. "You realize that the police may well come around and investigate now that the diamonds have been discovered."

Briana pushed aside thoughts of her mother. "But we gave them back," she said somewhat stupidly.

"The police will still investigate."

Ray swallowed hard. "Then they're going to find out about the million dollars," he said, sending a jolt through Briana.

Jarrod seemed to go on full alert. "What million dollars?"

"The one I stole from Howard's secret account."

"What the hell!"

"Just ignore him," Briana said quickly. "He doesn't know what he's saying."

Ray shook his head. "Honey, the guilt's been getting to me, and this has just made me decide to turn myself in to the police." He turned to Jarrod. "Remember that million dollars you loaned Briana to buy more property?" he said, making her inwardly groan.

Jarrod darted a look at her, and her eyes pleaded with him to nod. "Er—yes."

Ray then went on to explain how he'd taken the money for his wife's medical expenses. "I'll hand myself in to the police tomorrow." He glanced around the room. "I just want to spend one more night in the home I shared with Barbara."

Briana's heart tilted with pain. "Oh Dad," she whispered. "I'll come with you tomorrow. You won't be alone."

"Thank you, honey."

Jarrod cleared his throat. "Ray, embezzlement is embezzlement but there *were* extenuating circumstances. I know a good criminal lawyer who'll take on your case and hopefully will get you a lesser jail term."

At the mention of jail, Briana gave a small sob, but Ray squeezed her hand. "Honey, I committed a crime. I have to go to jail." He gave a forced smile. "You know I love you, but without your mother it doesn't really matter where I am."

"Oh, Dad, that's grief speaking."

"Maybe, but by the time I'm out of jail I might be over the worst of it." He smiled. "Look, you two get out of here. I've got a few things to do now."

A thought occurred to Briana. "Dad, you're not going to do anything silly, are you?"

His face softened. "I promise you I'm not. I just want some time alone."

"Okay." She hugged him then kissed his cheek. "I'll be back first thing in the morning."

"Fine."

"I'll be here for you, too, Ray," Jarrod said, and her father thanked him.

Briana hated that Jarrod had forced the issue, but she had to admit it was a relief to get it all out in the open. If only she could do the same with her feelings for Jarrod. If she could just tell him she loved him.

But that was never going to happen. It couldn't. She had to stay cool and calm in front of him. Jarrod had only ever wanted to bed her, not marry her. He'd told her from the beginning not to ask for more, so there was no way she would go back on her word. Not even after she told him about Patrick and the blackmail.

Once they were in the car, Jarrod looked at Briana in concern. "Are you okay?" he asked, realizing only now how hard this had been for her. The money must have weighed so heavily on her mind all this time.

She looked straight ahead, as if she knew she'd fall apart if she didn't. "Please take me home, Jarrod."

He waited a moment, a distinct feeling of unease rolling through him. Then he started up the engine and drove off, his thoughts turning to what had just taken place back there at Ray Davenport's house. He felt bad about Briana, not for pushing her about the diamonds—no, that had to be done. But for thinking the worst about her all this time.

Dammit, she didn't deserve all the rotten things he'd

thought about her from the beginning. He knew now she was a woman who could be trusted, and a woman who put her family before herself.

Unlike Marise.

Unlike his biological mother.

He owed Briana one hell of an apology. And he would give her one, too, just as soon as they were inside her apartment. He intended to make up for it all somehow—if she let him.

Only, when they arrived at her apartment building, she tried her old trick of telling him to just drop her off out front, but he wasn't having it this time. They needed to talk. And he needed to apologize.

She didn't say another word until they were inside her apartment. Then she stood in the middle of the living room and faced him, a cool look in her eyes. "You were wrong to force my father into a confession, Jarrod."

He couldn't back down. "If I hadn't, the police would have. And they'd have been much less considerate." He paused, then said in his defense, "Hell, I had no idea he was going to confess to embezzlement."

She flinched, then, "Perhaps you should have listened to me when I said to leave things alone. But you never listen to me, do you, Jarrod? It's always about what *you* want."

He inclined his head. "That's a fair comment," he admitted, and caught the look of surprise in her eyes before honing in to further the discussion. "So, the million dollars was actually for your father."

"Yes." Then out of the blue, her mouth began to

tremble. "And now I'm…going to lose…him." Tears bubbled up and overflowed down her cheeks.

Jarrod was at her side in an instant, pulling her into his arms, hugging her tight as she cried it all out. "Shhh. I'll do what I can to help him," he murmured, slipping her his clean handkerchief. He wondered if she'd cried much these last few months, or if she'd stayed strong for her father. More likely the latter, and he admired her for it. But today had to have been an emotional day for her, and things always caught up eventually.

He continued to hug her. "Shhh, Briana. You won't be alone. There are people who…care about you." And he realized he did. He just couldn't bring himself to be personal about it right now. He had to stand back and keep some semblance of detachment.

After a few more moments, she sniffed and pulled back, dabbing at her tears with the hanky, still looking so very beautiful. "There's something else."

His gut clenched tight as he let her leave his arms. "I'm beginning to not like surprises."

She sniffed again. "This one's about Patrick," she said, slamming his heart against his ribs. "He's blackmailing me."

Jarrod's head went back. "Blackmailing you? For what?"

"About the money my father stole from Howard. He figured it out, you see." She took a shuddering breath before continuing. "That's why he came to see me at the airport and why I was forced into signing that agreement. He was insisting I take him back as my business manager so that he could come to Hong Kong with me."

"The bastard!"

"And he wants everyone to think we're lovers again, just until he signs up one of the other models as a client." She hesitated then met his gaze full-on. "I agreed to him coming with me, but I refused to become his lover again." She shook her head emphatically, her eyelashes still damp from her tears. "Never."

Just the thought of Patrick forcing Briana into bed made him want to do violent things to the other man. Physically forcing a woman was one thing he would never do. And it wasn't like Patrick really wanted Briana anyway. Not like *he* did.

He swallowed hard. "Were you going to tell me the truth?"

Wariness clouded her eyes. "No," she said, and he swore. "Not even when I returned in two weeks. I couldn't." She gave a shaky sigh. "Anyway, the end of the month is almost here. It wouldn't have made any difference to you what I do after that."

"It would have mattered, Briana," he growled, admitting the truth. And that was the whole truth. He didn't want to let her go.

He never wanted to let her go. He wanted to keep her in his arms, safe by his side. Always.

Suddenly that thought grabbed him by the throat and had him heading for the door.

"Jarrod, stop! Where are you going?"

Anywhere. Nowhere. Just as long he was somewhere other than here. He needed time to think this all through.

He made himself focus, and he turned to briefly face her. "To see your ex-business manager," he said, letting the anger come. "He's not forcing you into anything, Briana."

She sighed. "It's no use, Jarrod. I signed a contract. Please don't make a scene."

"You can't be serious. You signed that contract under duress," he pointed out. "It wouldn't stand up in court and you know it."

She raised her chin. "Whether it does or it doesn't, I won't renege on the deal, Jarrod, no matter what you say. I gave my word. And if it's good enough for you—"

"Then you're a fool," he snapped, finding it hard to believe that she could even consider going away with Patrick when she didn't have to. He stilled. Perhaps that was the problem. Perhaps she *did* want to go away with Patrick, despite her protestations.

Something shifted in her expression. "Yes, I'm a fool, Jarrod," she said, a sudden catch in her voice. "A fool in love."

Jarrod felt like he'd just been poleaxed. She was in love with Patrick. The thought staggered him, squeezed his heart. And suddenly he knew why.

He loved her.

But he had lost her. She wanted another man. She *loved* another man. God, did he really have the strength to walk away from her? He shuddered inwardly. He had to. He loved her, but when it came right down to it, her happiness was what counted. Not his own.

"Then I hope you two will be very happy," he said, turning away before she could see the anguish that must be in his eyes. In seconds he'd loved and lost the most beautiful woman in the world. Beautiful in more ways than one.

"Oh Jarrod, now *you're* the fool. It's *you* I love. Not Patrick."

He felt his world rock as he spun back toward her. "What did you say?"

She stood her ground like someone expecting to be reprimanded, but defiant all the same. "I said I love you."

He was back at her side in an instant. "Darling, I love you, too. I'm so sorry for what I've put you through."

Her heart stopped. "What?"

He put his hand under her chin and looked into her eyes. "I've only just realized I love you, Briana. Right now when I thought I'd lost you to Patrick."

Oh my. Was she dreaming?

"Then I have to be grateful to Patrick for giving you to me," she murmured, slipping her hands around his neck, enjoying the freedom of touching him with love.

Jarrod's hands slid down to her waist and pulled her lower half close against him. "No," he growled. "We don't owe him a thing. Patrick can go to hell for all I care."

"Jarrod!" Briana said, pretending to be shocked at his words, but more surprised by his arousal against her stomach. But she felt the same way about Patrick. He didn't deserve any consideration. He would have used her if he could and not given a damn.

"Forget Patrick," Jarrod said. "We'll deal with him tomorrow. Together. I'm sure the police will be very interested in his attempts at blackmail."

"Yes." She would report him, if only to stop him doing the same thing to someone else. Another woman may not have someone like Jarrod.

All at once the air softened with love. "And you're not going on assignment to Asia by yourself either," Jarrod said gruffly. "I'm rearranging my schedule so I can go with you."

For once she loved his high-handedness. "No argument from me," she agreed, just before he slid his mouth over hers and kissed her hard.

Eventually they came up for air. "But for now—" He swept her up in his arms and headed to the bedroom. "I think we need some practice."

"Practice?"

"For our honeymoon."

She gave a small gasp. "Are you asking me to marry you, Jarrod Hammond?"

He stopped to look down at her and she caught her breath at the sheer love in his eyes. "Darling, only special people get to come inside my heart and stay forever. And you're the most special person of all."

"Oh, Jarrod," she whispered, his words making her heart turn over and over until she thought it would never stop.

And then she realized she didn't want it to stop. Every beat of her heart would always be for him. Always and forever.

* * * * *

Watch for the next
DIAMONDS DOWN UNDER *release,*
SATIN & A SCANDALOUS AFFAIR
by Jan Colley,
available in April 2008
from Silhouette Desire.